MARRIAGE MADE IN HELL...

"The prosecutor is going to suggest you went home, killed Hal, and then went to Sylvia's."

"But I didn't! It's not true."

"And our job is to make sure people see that you didn't kill him. We're going to have to do better than saying you were driving around for two hours trying to think. So let's start there. You're going to have to remember that drive."

"Andrew, I haven't been arrested. Nobody has accused me of anything. Does a person have to prove she's innocent?"

"Let's call it a day then. But I want you to try to reconstruct the time between leaving the club and getting to Sylvia's. You weren't drunk, were you?"

"I've never been drunk a day in my life."

"Do me a favor, Pauline. Don't say that under oath."

———————————— ★ ————————————

RALPH McINERNY

AN ANDREW BROOM MYSTERY

BODY AND SOIL

WORLDWIDE.

TORONTO · NEW YORK · LONDON · PARIS
AMSTERDAM · STOCKHOLM · HAMBURG
ATHENS · MILAN · TOKYO · SYDNEY

BODY AND SOIL

A Worldwide Mystery/January 1991

This edition is reprinted by arrangement with Atheneum
Publishers, an imprint of Macmillan Publishing
Company.

ISBN 0-373-26063-6

For Bev and John Krucek

ONE

LEO BARANY worked out of the ancestral home in Privett, a trilevel about a mile and a half north of town on the Wabash Road. The house stood 150 yards off the road, on a little rise, and was reached by a driveway his father had never gotten around to blacktopping. That made it hell in winter and not much better in this kind of August weather, dry as a bone, the dust settling for five minutes after Barany drove in. Sometimes he would sit in the car for several minutes before getting out, the windows closed tight, listening to himself on tape, waiting for the air to clear.

When it did, he would lean forward and look at the house. He was lucky to have the place, but he knew better than to tell himself that. This was the house to which they had moved when he was fifteen, from what had truly been the ancestral home farther back on the property, gone now, having made way for another acre or two of soybeans. His father had built the trilevel with minimum help from others—from Uncle Jim on the odd weekend, and Barany's mother, of course. The old man was proud as a rooster when it was done. He put in lawn and Leo took care of that; he also put in flower beds, with mixed results. Leo's parents had not had much time for flowers and shrubs after breaking their asses on those miserable thirty acres and also holding down jobs in town most of the time. What did it mean to be a farmer anymore?

The house his old man tore down after they moved into
the trilevel had been built in 1885 by Patrick Devere and
had proudly looked out over eight hundred acres, including two densely wooded areas and a small lake which
was now a hazard on the Walnut Grove Golf Course. The
Devere farm had gradually grown larger over the years,
until the Depression, when Grandpa Devere lost all but
thirty acres. Leo Barany had grown up listening to his
mother talk about how it had been when she was a girl.
He felt almost like deposed royalty, and he inherited from
his mother a sullen resentment. For Mrs. Barany, October 12 was not Columbus Day, but the anniversary of the
foreclosing of the mortgage on the Devere farm. On that
day his mother wore black, but his father wore a sar-
donic grin. The old man had not liked the suggestion that
if her family had not fallen on hard times she would never
have married a man like him.

After he finished the trilevel, Barany senior had the old
Devere place torn down. To hell with tradition, they
needed the land for planting. From the age of fifteen, Leo
dreamed of leaving the house his father had built. He
would go away and become rich and buy back every
goddam acre Grandpa Devere had lost and that would
show the sonsofbitches.

Well, he had gone away, but he had not become rich.
He hadn't really tried, which was a long story in itself,
and he came back to take possession of the trilevel when
his parents were reported missing in Florida.

They had never been found.

They were buried in the backyard, beneath the little
sheet-metal storage shed his old man had bought for the
rider mower. The shed had a concrete floor now.

Barany could live in the house, all right, so long as he
paid the taxes, but he'd have to wait for anything else

coming his way from his father, and nothing he could say would change it.

"Ask a lawyer," Howlett said. "I don't make the laws, I just enforce them. Someone missing has to be declared dead before the will can be probated, and in this state that means five years."

"But they were reported missing in Florida."

"Maybe they're missing *from* Florida and not *in* it," Howlett said with a sly rustic grin.

Barany let it go. For a week he worried, wondering if Howlett suspected something. But he decided that was impossible.

Hire a lawyer? With what? If Howlett was right, he wouldn't get anything and would be unable to pay the lawyer. If Howlett was wrong, the lawyer would no doubt descend on the property like a vulture. Barany had read somewhere, maybe in *Reader's Digest,* that a shrewd lawyer could eat an estate alive, and legally too.

So Leo Barany had to wait. He couldn't sell the house and he didn't want to rent it. He wasn't worried about the storage shed, not with that concrete floor he had laid, but there was no point in taking chances.

Howlett's remark proved to be one he couldn't forget. And anyway, where the hell would he go?

Nights he would sit in the breezeway his old man had built where you caught the scent coming in over the fields, a sweet sad smell that brought back all Leo's boyhood longing. He could look down the driveway winding toward the Wabash Road and recall how he had dreamt of leaving once and for all, shaking the dust from his shoes and never looking back.

He had been a runner-up for a Merit scholarship when he graduated from high school in Wyler, the next town to the north, and that had got him a state scholarship to

Purdue, where he majored in English, a way of thumbing his nose at the engineers who made up the majority. He got a graduate fellowship to the University of Minnesota, but somehow during the cold Minneapolis winters the rising line of his academic career flattened, ran parallel to the earth for a year or so, and then, after he failed two of his written candidacy examinations, went into a nose-dive from which it never recovered.

He had dreamt of a professor's life, lecturing to enraptured students, contributing insightful gems to PMLA and *Notes & Queries*. Like his fellow graduate students, he had been grading his professors for years, and finally they had graded him and said he could not belong to the club. Home to Indiana? The thought of driving up the Wabash Road to the trilevel and explaining to his parents that he would not after all become a college professor was more than he could bear. So he created the fiction that he had hit a snag in his dissertation, that the writing was not going well, and cited vague research problems. His parents did not understand well enough to know what he was saying, but the old man guessed he had bombed out and said so.

But that was after Barany had despaired of supporting himself by the work he was willing to take in Minneapolis and had made the momentous decision to return to Indiana. What had been insufficient in Minneapolis turned out to be good enough in Privett, so he had gone on with telephone sales. He was proud of his voice. Despite the fact that he had no chance now of ever becoming a professor, Leo recorded imaginary classroom lectures on cassettes and listened to himself with critical ear. God, he would have been good. In the meantime, his voice was his meal ticket by way of telephone sales.

That is how it started with Mrs. Stanfield.

He kept a record of his calls, that being required by Magazine Publishers' Information Enterprise, or Magpie as Barany sardonically thought of it, a record of the sales as well as of the majority that said no in various ways ranging from the polite to the infuriating.

Barany understood the annoyance, up to a point. Someone involved in telesales was not immune to the approach himself. Barany too had answered the phone only to receive a pitch for something he did not want—aluminum siding, driveway resurfacing, property in the Ozarks—and had felt the impulse to tell the caller what he could do with his bargain. So he half expected to be insulted when he settled down with his phone to put in a three-to-four-hour stretch offering incredible subscription bargains. His approach was to congratulate the person on having been selected for a free subscription to *Time* (if the phone was answered by a man) or *People* (if it was answered by a woman). Almost never did the person hang up immediately, and Leo got well into his prepared remarks before the supposed winner began to smell a rat. Those who fell for it never objected to the fact that they had to subscribe to two other magazines in order to receive their free subscription.

Of course, lots of people—most really—changed their attitude as soon as they realized that the gift they had been awarded would cost them considerably if they wished to claim it. Then, in a variety of ways, they brought the conversation to a close. Sometimes abruptly, by simply hanging up. Fair enough. Sometimes with a cold expression of lack of interest, but thanking him before the line went dead. Others were angered by his effort to deceive them, and this anger was expressed in degrees of intensity. Barany had been insulted profanely, sometimes wittily, even tearfully. He had hung up on a few people himself. Two can play at that game.

But there were some disgruntled people he could not hang up on. Sometimes the reaction went beyond insult. Early in the game he had once made the fundamental mistake of giving his own number to a potential customer who asked if he could call back in ten minutes. Barany had said he would return the call. No, the man insisted. He must give his number. Of course, if he did not want to make a sale... Barany gave the man his number.

For weeks afterward he was called at the most ungodly hours and offered square inches of tundra in the Klondike, fishing rights in the Sudan, a holiday to Haiti to begin when he was met by an armored car at the airport. The sonofabitch had been relentless. But Barany had finally silenced him.

A guy named Slattery.

He too was buried in the yard behind the trilevel. Slattery had been the worst—until Mrs. Stanfield. Now when Barany sat in the breezeway in the evening nursing a can of beer, he thought of how he would settle his account with Mrs. Pauline Stanfield.

TWO

ON THE EIGHTH GREEN of the Walnut Grove Golf Course, Hal Stanfield stood looking back toward the tee while with the index finger of his right hand he dramatically ticked off the strokes he had taken. Portrait of a golfer in the act of lying. Andrew Broom winked at his nephew Gerald and silently mouthed the word "six."

"Six!" said Hal Stanfield, his reconstruction of the crime completed. "I'll take a six."

And "take" was the operative word. He had struck his ball at least nine times after his drive—with a club, that is. He had also kicked it out from behind a tree, reset it on a pinched pyramid of sand in a fairway bunker, and considered the final three feet separating it from the hole a gimme.

"Six it is," Andrew Broom said heartily. "Gerald?"

"Four."

"I thought you birdied."

"Nope. You beat me."

"You had a three?" Hal Stanfield exclaimed in wondering tones. For a moment he seemed about to ask himself for a recount of his own performance on the hole. "Damned if I don't know why you didn't become a pro, Andrew."

"Then I couldn't have been your lawyer, Hal."

"I wish you'd give me some counsel about my game."

Andrew Broom shook his head. "The last thing anyone really wants is advice on his game while he's playing."

"Try me."

Andrew looked at him for a moment. "Okay. Keep your head down."

"I do!"

"There, what did I tell you?"

"Are you saying I'm looking up when I come through?"

On the ninth tee, driving last, Hal made a heroic effort to keep his head down and sent the ball out 150 yards before it bent abruptly to the left and ended in the rough. He was overjoyed nonetheless. He hadn't hit a drive that long all summer. They arrived at the clubhouse with Hal in a great mood, even though he double-bogied nine and admitted it. He was all for going right to the tenth tee and continuing their round without a break.

Andrew Broom shook his head. "I have a phone call to make, Hal. I told you that."

"Don't you ever just relax and enjoy life?"

Coming from Hal Stanfield, that question had all the makings of a good joke. If any man failed to relax and enjoy life, that man was Hal Stanfield.

Uncle Andrew went off to phone and Gerald was left with Stanfield. The phone call was a ruse, the idea being to leave Gerald alone with the client to establish an independent relationship and eventually ease some of the Stanfield legal business off his uncle's shoulders. But it was Stanfield who seemed determined to make use of Andrew's absence.

"How do you like Wyler after—how long is it—a year, Gerald?"

It had been six months. "I like it."

"Not too dull for you?"

"Andrew's practice is as various as he claimed. I'm becoming far more of a lawyer here than I would have in Chicago."

"That was the choice?"

"Yes." Gerald had a vision of the two floors in the 1st National Bank Building that housed the several regiments of lawyers he would have joined as an obscure foot soldier. How would these past six months have gone in that atmosphere?

Hal said, "I would have chosen Chicago."

Gerald smiled. "Never argue with a client" was one of the many precepts he had picked up from Andrew. The truth was, he didn't give a damn what Hal Stanfield thought.

"Wyler," Stanfield said in tragic tones, shaking his head. "What a Godawful dull town."

"You've done pretty well here." Stanfield's insurance agency, founded by his father, dwarfed anything in Wyler and for miles around. Stanfield was a principal stockholder in the Wyler Clinic—the only one with a bigger piece was Andrew Broom—had an estatelike home in the part of Wyler where Andrew lived, had a condominium in Florida, and was in residence there or in far-flung hotels around the globe for a significant portion of every year. It was difficult to see how he could have done better.

"This place is bad enough for a married man," Hal Stanfield said. "What the hell is it like for a bachelor?"

"I've been kept too busy to notice," Gerald said, not quite truly. Hal Stanfield had assumed the expression of a middle-aged roué.

"Let me give you some advice, Gerald. First, put off marriage as long as you can. Second, get as much as you can now."

Did everyone over fifty have a set of precepts he wanted to pass on to the young? Hal Stanfield's advice was considerably different from Uncle Andrew's. Gerald nodded in masculine camaraderie.

"The biggest mistake I ever made was marrying at twenty-four."

From what Gerald knew of Mrs. Stanfield, he did not see how postponing the marriage would have made it any less of a disaster.

"Did you ever read Chaucer?" Andrew, surprisingly, had asked when briefing Gerald on Hal Stanfield.

"If I did, I forgot it."

"I think it's *The Miller's Tale*. It doesn't matter. Hal is the classically comic husband. A shrewish wife who may or may not be faithful. He knows he's the butt of jokes because of Pauline."

"Why does he stay with her?"

Andrew gave Gerald a long look. "Divorce? This is Wyler, Indiana, where marriages are for keeps." He seemed to be daring Gerald to think of Dorothy and her fatal dalliance with Dr. Lister. Marriage to Susannah had rejuvenated Andrew, put new fire in his belly. The firm's business had increased by 20 percent in the time Gerald had been there.

"Would you handle it if he wanted one?"

Andrew shook his head. "You would."

"I've never handled a divorce."

"Well, the Stanfields never got one before—what's the difference? The main problem would be to sort out what goes to whom."

"But you don't think he would actually try to get a divorce?"

"Probably not. But taking them at their word may wake them up."

That is when Uncle Andrew had told Gerald they would be golfing with Hal Stanfield at Walnut Grove.

The course was a dream, with long narrow fairways whose strategically placed traps put such a premium on accuracy that playing the course well depended a good deal on settling for shorter drives and as many iron shots as possible. Going for broke at Walnut Grove almost always ended up as going broke. Not even the negative briefing about Hal Stanfield could have dissuaded Gerald from taking this opportunity to play the course again in company with his uncle. Golfing with others was simply several notches below golfing with Andrew, who was pound for pound the best amateur golfer Gerald had ever seen.

And now here he sat with Hal Stanfield enjoying a beer on the Walnut Grove clubhouse patio while Uncle Andrew was probably having a Diet Coke at the bar inside. Hovering in the heated air like a buzzing insect was Hal Stanfield's discontent. He was a man impossible to like. Self-indulgent, a cheater at golf and thus most likely at life, no prize as a husband, so who cared if he had gotten an unsatisfying wife?

"Some mistakes can be corrected," Hal mused. "Others cannot. The important ones fall in the second class."

"Like marriage?"

"You read me right. What has Andrew told you?"

"Nothing." That was in conformity with another precept of Uncle Andrew's. Always let the client give you the information he thinks is important. Put out of your mind everything you have heard up to that point.

"Bullshit."

He answered with a smile. Never argue.

"My marriage is legendary in this town, Gerald. Both Pauline and I know we made a fundamental mistake."

"There are legal remedies," Gerald said, but his heart was not in it. The prospect of representing this pouting, weak-chinned cheater was abhorrent.

"In order to divorce we would have to unweave financial threads that have been intertwined for two generations. I do not need your uncle to tell me it cannot be done."

"Is that what he told you?"

"I understand finance at least as well as he does. It is an impossibly tangled web."

Did he intend the allusion?

"A cardinal tenet of Broom and Broom is that no legal problem is insoluble."

"This isn't a legal problem."

"Ownership of assets is a legal problem."

"You wouldn't say that if you got a look at things."

Gerald glanced toward the clubhouse. No sign of Andrew. He shrugged. "Since I won't be getting such a look, we'll never know."

"You think you could do it?"

"Not as a challenge to my ingenuity. There would have to be a purpose."

It was left there. Hal finished his beer, Gerald left half of his in the clear plastic cup, and Andrew emerged as if he had showered and had a nap. Whatever, he took the back nine like Nicklaus on his best day, breaking the course record for the back nine and tying it for eighteen. To make it worse, he sauntered from the eighteenth green as if he were fully capable of going right out and repeating the feat.

"Drinks are on me," he said magnanimously.

"What the hell for?" Hal asked. His head was soaking wet and his sweat-stained shirt clung to his bloated torso. He took the offer of a free drink as an added insult. Even with outrageous cheating, he had carded 111 for eighteen.

Gerald explained that Andrew had just broken the course record for the back nine.

"Who held it before?"

Andrew Broom, as it turned out. Hal Stanfield said that he would be damned if he would celebrate a man's beating him and ordered the first of what would be for him four sizable Rob Roys. Andrew nursed a martini; Gerald had a beer. On the third drink Hal Stanfield said that what Gerald had suggested earlier made him think seriously of maybe filing for divorce. He said it loudly enough so that everyone in the bar must have heard him, but only a few were distracted by the announcement.

"Good idea," Andrew said, avoiding Gerald's eye.

"I would want you to handle it."

"We would be happy to."

"I'm talking to your nephew."

"I should think so. He is the one who will handle it."

"I'm serious, Andrew."

"So am I."

Hal sipped his drink and shook his head. "I wonder how Pauline would take it."

"How do you mean?"

"With you two on my side, she'd have to bring in someone from out of town."

"I don't see why."

"Oh, come on, Andrew. As far as first-rank law goes, you're it in Wyler."

"Pauline has already spoken to me, Hal."

"How do you mean?"

"About the divorce."

"We've been talking about it for years."

"This was two days ago. I agreed to represent her."

THREE

PAULINE STANFIELD left it to Andrew Broom to tell Hal that the years of talk were over, she intended to file for divorce and, as she told her friend Silvia Wood, take the sonofabitch for all he was worth. No point in saying that to Andrew; he meant for this to be polite and genteel, a friendly divorce, and maybe it would be, if Hal played ball, but since the chances of that happening were nil, Pauline was certain that, in the end, even Andrew Broom would go for the jugular, reduce Hal to penury, and establish Pauline as independent and wealthy.

"Then what?" Silvia asked, sinking sharp little teeth into the olive she had plucked from her drink.

"Then I head for Acapulco, my dear. And you can come along."

"Is it safe?"

"As long as you don't drink the water."

"Then it's safe," said Silvia.

Pauline laughed, but she was not deceived. Silvia was a good drinking companion, but she never got drunk. She was lots of fun, which is why Pauline liked her. She liked the brashness, the irreverence, the assumption that her looks and brains made her the equal of any man. And she was right.

Silvia had married at eighteen, a hunk of a truck driver she met when she was a counter girl at a diner west of her Iowa hometown. That marriage had meant one trip to Chicago, half a year in a furnished room in Joliet, Illinois, just being there for him when he got in off the road.

She sat there reading the *National Enquirer* and "other great books of western culture" until one day she got religion.

"Well, not religion. There was this big church up the street from where the room was, Catholic, a cathedral, and it had this chalk white statue out front, maybe St. Francis, and I thought, at least I think I thought this, he's not just theirs, I meant St. Francis, he's everybody's. I had seen a movie about Francis. Anyway, it made it all less strange, and one day I went inside and sat down and had a good talk with God. Did he really mean for me to go on sitting in that empty room waiting for Emil and then spending two days nonstop in bed with him before he went off again? It wasn't a marriage. He didn't want kids. Anyway, God and I agreed that I should get out of there, so I did."

Pauline could listen to Silvia by the hour, she was never quite sure why. Oh, the stories were interesting enough, whether or not they were completely true, but it wasn't just diversion. Silvia's escapades stood for all the chances Pauline had missed by being married to Hal. Marriage was Hal, and she meant it the way it sounded. She had been truer to him than he had been to her, but her few lapses were just that, momentary relief from the long unending Blah that was life with Hal Stanfield in Wyler, Indiana.

"Honey, it's a nice town," Silvia would say when Pauline got going on it. "Believe me, I have seen far worse."

"And far better."

Silvia conceded the point. "Isn't there an old saying, 'You never appreciate what you got.' I'll be frank with you, Pauline, and this may cost me a trip to Acapulco. If I was married to Hal Stanfield, I would make the best of it because the best is plenty. I mean, look at you. You dress like a model, you live in this house—"

"Silvia, whatever can be bought, I can afford without him. At least half of what we have is mine."

"Okay, okay. But money isn't enough. Sure, you can go to Acapulco, places like that, you can afford the posh hotels, the clubs, and some local José will look like the most handsome guy you ever saw and your wish is his command."

"Go on, go on," Pauline urged.

Silvia laughed. "I don't say there's nothing to be said for it, but, Pauline, it's a vacation, it's not a way of life. Give it ten days, two weeks, okay, that's time off for bad behavior, but you can't make a career of it, go on to Hawaii or wherever, one chain of parties. Believe me, I tried. Even when it's going good, do you know what it is? It's lonely. Men you meet like that are either robots, blow-up dolls that do your will, or they are tourists too and you can meet those anywhere."

"Have you been back to church talking with God?"

"Don't laugh, Pauline. When I meet him, I want to be on speaking terms."

"You don't think he'll disapprove of you?"

"Of what I've done? Sure."

It was too much for Pauline. In any case, she did not want to pursue it. This was not an unfamiliar side of Silvia—the repentant sinner, the advocate of the status quo. If Silvia had claimed they could hop a plane and fly into a wholly different world, everything perfect, Pauline would not have believed her. It was the mention of the flaws in paradise that made her descriptions authentic.

Five years ago Silvia had come to Wyler and opened the first of her unisex hairdressing and tanning parlors. There were now three in Wyler and another in Privett.

Silvia was doing well. Andrew Broom referred to her admiringly as an entrepreneur. Silvia actually beamed when she heard this.

"I hope you don't have designs on Andrew Broom, Silvia."

"Ha. When I asked him to represent me, he turned me over to Gerald."

"Thank God he's on my side now."

"When will you file?"

"Next week."

"He thinks you're doing the right thing?"

Pauline started to answer, then stopped. When she spoke, it was more slowly. "I don't know. But he will represent me in the divorce. If he had taken Hal's side, I don't know what I would have done. So he must think he can work things out. Believe me, Silvia, it is largely a matter of making us both believe we are getting our fair share. I brought a lot to this marriage and I intend to take it with me. But beyond that, I don't know what Andrew Broom thinks. I never have."

"What was his first wife like?"

"Maybe if you had known Dorothy you wouldn't be so sure that staying on in Wyler is the answer."

"Why wasn't he suspected when her car blew up?"

"It was his car, not hers. He was the one meant to die. There was never any question of that. Besides, Andrew would have killed the man, not his wife. Dr. Lister committed suicide, so that was that."

"He married again and lived happily ever after?"

"So it seems."

"His secretary?"

"That's right. And she still is, with a fancier title, but she runs his office. I don't like her, but you have to admire her."

From outside came the purr of the lawn tractor, and the smell of freshly cut grass drifted to them on the patio. Pauline was seized by an intimation of peace and, for the moment it lasted, thought her life was good as it was, more than just good. She loved this house.

"Who will act as Hal's lawyer?"

Pauline just stared at her friend. "Good question." She broke into a smile. "I said how I would feel if Andrew was on Hal's side—well, it has to be the same for Hal. He will be furious."

"What if he brings in someone from Chicago?"

"It would be a waste of money. Andrew Broom is not in Wyler, Indiana, because he could not have made it in Chicago or New York or Dallas."

"Why is he here?"

"He actually prefers it. He chose to make his life here, and so did Gerald, his nephew."

"All I know, if I couldn't have Andrew, I'm glad I have Gerald. If I had known all the problems involved in running a business, I might have settled for another husband instead."

"Honey, you don't know what problems are."

Another drink? Why not. Hal was off golfing somewhere and wouldn't be back until late.

"You don't sound like a woman about to get a divorce."

"Why not?"

"Your day swings around what your husband does."

It was her Achilles' heel, no doubt of that; it was what
had been true all her life. She could be discontent with
what she had, but she had never been able to imagine a
life that was truly her own. Of course, for years she
hadn't even noticed this. Her life had been arranged
through childhood, then she was sent off to St. Mary's of
the Lake, after which Daddy told her she was going to
Northwestern. She had applied to three places, following instructions, and had wanted to go east because some
of her friends had, but Daddy said Northwestern and that
was that. Even now, determined to leave Hal, she found
herself thinking of going off on trips with Silvia.

Well, who wanted to do things completely on their
own? Besides, her friendship with Silvia was at least in
part a thumb in Hal's eye.

"She's a tramp," he growled, and Pauline smiled, Silvia having told her of the big move Hal had made on her.

"She is very successful."

"What the hell is a tanning parlor, anyway? Do they
give massages?"

"Why don't you go see?"

"If I want a tan, I'll get it the old-fashioned way,
playing golf."

Now, sipping a fresh drink with Silvia, smelling the cut
grass from the shade of the porch, Pauline wondered
what Hal would do without her. He might like to fool
around, but he needed a wife to give orders to. No doubt
he would marry again.

She tried telling herself no one would have him, but she
knew that wasn't true. From many points of view he
would be a good catch. He still had some looks—granted

a pot, but pots of money too. Money could make up for lots of defects.

"I was thinking," she said to Silvia. "I suppose Hal will marry again."

"Maybe you will too."

"Not on your life! If I regain my freedom, I don't intend to lose it. Still, it's a funny thought, Hal married to someone else."

Silvia nodded and her eyes drifted speculatively over the new-mown lawn.

FOUR

ON THE DRIVE from the golf course, with Gerald at the wheel, Andrew Broom tried not to think of Pauline and Hal Stanfield. The truth was that they reminded him of the couple he and his first wife, Dorothy, had been. Like Pauline, Dorothy had brought money to their marriage, and there were times when he thought she had unconsciously resented his success.

He brushed the thought away. He liked psychological explanations even less in real life than he did in court. People do what people do for the reasons people give. In the end, that was the best way to understand oneself and others.

Dorothy had fallen in love with Lister at the clinic and all too quickly their only solution seemed to be to get rid of Andrew. Well, the plan backfired, both Dorothy and her lover were dead, and Andrew had ended up with Susannah. No point in comparing Dorothy and Susannah. He had loved Dorothy for years and now he loved Susannah.

He had learned from that episode that when people say they can't stand it anymore, they may very well mean it. And if they do and they can't just walk away, chances are they'll do something desperate.

"Stanfield took it pretty well," Gerald said.

"Why not? He's got a good lawyer."

"What's the ethics of this, Andrew? Do we stop talking about the Stanfields?"

"It will be pretty difficult negotiating a settlement if we don't talk. No, you look out for your client and I'll look out for mine."

"So we're competitors rather than partners."

Andrew smiled. "For the nonce."

"And you think you can whip my ass?"

"I think you better be sure I don't."

Gerald pulled into a *NO PARKING* space in front of the Hoosier Towers. "Why are you coming back to the office?"

It was after five o'clock, but twilight was hours away in this Indiana summer. "I'm going over to the courthouse and have a talk with Hogan."

"I could drop you there."

Andrew shook his head. "I want to stop at the office first."

Old Bartlett was already at his pulpit in the lobby, keeping an eye on those leaving the building, since no one was coming in. Andrew signed in, momentarily doubting the need for this procedure, but only momentarily. When he worked nights, he wanted to know who else was in the building. For one thing, he had controlling interest in the Towers and the twin concerns of liability and security. The tenants accepted the practice even though they were hit for a portion of Bartlett's salary. For another thing, it had been a way to help Bartlett.

Bartlett in uniform became officious, and until Andrew signed his name in the book on the pulpitlike desk, he might have been a stranger to the nightguard. His was the first name on the page. There would be others. The air-conditioned silence of the Hoosier Towers drew tenants back in the evening during these hot summer months.

"Mr. Stanfield got here before five, so he didn't have to sign in."

"Stanfield's here?"

"He said he would wait in your office."

Andrew Broom wore a poker face across the lobby, and when an elevator opened and emptied, he stood aside patiently, but when he was in the car and had hit *12,* he swore aloud.

"That sonofabitch," he told the empty elevator. "How did he beat Gerald here?"

He reached out and pressed *11* and at that floor got out and took the stairs to the top floor. He eased open the door. There was no sign of Stanfield. Had Susannah been able to think of a lie persuasive enough to get rid of him?

Susannah looked up sheepishly when he came in, but he gave her his biggest smile and a kiss besides.

"Hal Stanfield is here."

He nodded. "Bartlett told me."

Her lips silently formed a sentence. "I tried."

He kissed her again. "Is everything set up with Hogan?"

"Whenever you want."

"As soon as I finish here."

Hal, of course, had gone into Andrew's office, where he stood at the windows looking out over Wyler. He did not turn at the sound of the door opening and closing.

"You've got a real Berchtesgaden here, Andrew."

"The man who owned Berchtesgaden was a loser."

Hal turned and at first was just a silhouette. "Andrew, you're my lawyer, not Pauline's. You're not going to represent her in a divorce. And I don't like your trying to palm me off on Gerald Rowan, even if he is your nephew."

"Sit down, Hal."

"I couldn't say this in front of the boy."

"The 'boy' was offered jobs by the three top law firms in the city of Chicago. When I persuaded him to become my partner, it was the best thing I've done for this town in years. Of course, we'll have to dissolve the partnership. You're in good hands, Hal."

"I'm the insurance man, remember?" Hal Stanfield was very calm. He looked at Andrew for a full minute. "There isn't going to be any divorce."

"You mean you're going to fight it?"

"I don't want you to file any action for Pauline."

Andrew sat forward and opened the cigarette box on his desk. They were there for Susannah. If she wanted to smoke, she should do it in public; at least she shouldn't hide it from him. He removed a cigarette and picked up the lighter.

"You don't smoke," Hal said, his tone almost shocked.

"I know." He snapped the lighter and brought it toward the cigarette, his eyes on the mesmerized Hal Stanfield as he did so. He inhaled deeply, nearly blacking out, but managing to conceal it. "I hope you don't mind if I smoke."

"Mind! I'd like to join you."

Andrew pushed the box toward Hal, who drew back as from temptation. Andrew took another drag, the smoke bitter on his tongue. He did not inhale it. He wasn't enjoying this, but Hal had lost his peremptory tone if not his line of thought.

"It hit me as I was driving back to Wyler, Andy. I don't want to break up with Pauline."

"You should be telling her this."

"I intend to."

"And she has to tell me not to file suit."

"Goddam it, Andy. *I'm* telling you. You're my lawyer."

"On this matter Gerald is your lawyer."

"I don't want him!"

"That's up to you, of course. Then we won't dissolve the partnership."

The door opened and Susannah looked in, doubtless having heard Hal shout. "There's still coffee on," she said.

"You want some coffee, Hal?"

"I want a drink."

"Can't oblige you there, I'm afraid. I'm due at the courthouse."

"At this hour?"

"To see a client. Duff Hogan."

"That sonofabitch. Sorry, Susannah. What's got into you, Andrew, representing that degenerate, and trying to foist Gerald off on me while you help Pauline take me to the cleaners. Susannah, you better have a talk with this man. He's becoming unglued."

"I might get the chance if clients didn't pop in at all hours and demand to see him."

"Pauline and I are not getting a divorce," Hal told her.

"I'm glad to hear that," Susannah said.

"You better talk to Pauline before you tell everybody else, Hal."

"Andrew, I held back because of your nephew, but I won't because of Susannah. She knows everything anyway. Forget anything else I ever said. Pauline and I are not going to break up."

He seemed satisfied that he had done what he had come to do.

"I'll be waiting to hear from her, Hal."

"You will. Don't worry. But you've already got the message."

Susannah showed him out, if only to make certain he had gone. When she came back, she walked right into Andrew's arms and he held her tightly.

"I really did try to get rid of him, Andrew."

"He's not easy to handle."

"Can you handle him?"

"I have turned him over to Gerald."

"Is that fair to Gerald?"

He stepped back and looked into her eyes. Did she have a point? But Gerald's apprenticeship involved seeing that the law is never merely routine, not even in Wyler, Indiana. The Stanfield breakup would require a financial settlement that would acquaint Gerald with a significant segment of local business, banking, and ownership. Working with Hal would be a lesson in itself, since Stanfield found it difficult to confide completely in anyone, even his lawyer. His involvement in the new chain of hairdressing and tanning salons was something Andrew had found out about only accidentally, when Welter at the bank asked him about Hallelujah Enterprises.

"What's the nature of your interest?" Andrew asked carefully.

"It's a loan request and Hal Stanfield insists we give it."

"Conflict of interest?"

"He doesn't see it that way. The money he has in it is at second remove and he argues that all but cuts him out of operational decisions."

Welter wore an omega of wrinkles on his forehead. He twisted a plastic tube he held and anointed his lips. Permanent chapped lips were his affliction, doubtless due to licking them in greedy anticipation. The banker was un-

aware that he had just told Andrew something he did not
know and really had no right to know. It wasn't the first
time Hal Stanfield had kept his lawyer in the dark about
his business dealings. Andrew wondered who was doing
the legal work. Of course he was angry. Choosing to
represent Pauline rather than Hal in their threatened
breakup was related to that.

But he was not punishing Gerald.

"Susannah, call Cleary and tell him I'm on my way."

"Do you want me along?"

"Unless you're busy."

She made a face, put her arm through his, and
marched him from the office.

FIVE

DUFF HOGAN was twenty-seven years old, five feet four inches high, and weighed 195 bare-ass naked when Cleary checked him into the jail. The stripping was to make certain Duff had no concealed weapons, and when Cleary said he wanted Duff thoroughly searched, he meant it, duff and all. Landers put on the rubber gloves for this, but that didn't mean he didn't hate Cleary for it. As for Sheriff Cleary himself, he had avoided breathing the same air as Hogan since bail was refused and he had ended up with a pervert as a permanent guest in the county jail.

"Why the hell don't you put him in the hospital?" Landers asked.

"He's not sick."

"Who says?"

"The clinic. They gave him every test there is. He's cleaner than you are, Herb."

"The hell he is."

"How you gonna catch anything anyway?" Cleary asked suggestively.

"I'll tell you one thing, I'm feeding that bastard on paper plates with plastic silverware."

"Plastic silverware?"

"Utensils."

"What's he like?"

"Hogan? What do you think he's like?"

"Does he ever talk?"

"Not to me, he doesn't."

Cleary quit teasing Landers. The weirdos never looked like weirdos, that seemed to be the rule. Duff Hogan might have been the Pillsbury doughboy in the TV ads. He just didn't seem to be the kind of man who would go for boys; despite his age, he looked like a little kid himself. Maybe nobody would have thought Duff was responsible for the death of little Larry Moss if he hadn't confessed. Then all kinds of kids said he was the man who had done one damned thing after another. Yoder the prosecutor sat in on the questioning, sure they were dealing with a mass murderer even though Cleary pointed out that there would have to be a mass of people dead or missing in order for Hogan to be a mass murderer.

"As I remember, Sheriff, there is at least one missing person."

"Slattery is a grown man, not a boy."

Every time Cleary lit another cigarette, Yoder watched as if he were witnessing a crime, but the smoke was meant to cleanse the air of Hogan's germs so far as the sheriff was concerned. Maybe Yoder would have been able to pin every unsolved crime in the county on Hogan if Andrew Broom hadn't decided to represent Duff.

Cleary didn't understand it. Broom hadn't been appointed by the court, he had volunteered, but if Hogan knew how lucky he was, he gave no sign of it. Far from it. In court, when Broom pleaded him innocent, Hogan stood up.

"I did it. I killed that boy."

Judge Teufel threatened to hold him in contempt if he spoke again.

"I already hold you in contempt," Hogan said in his velvety voice. You would have thought he was from Brown County in southern Indiana the way he talked.

Broom managed to deflect the judge's wrath, which was not easy. Teufel was already on his dignity, never content with the treatment he got from lawyers or peace officers or the public at large. The governor who appointed him, Bremen, had survived charges of corruption and was now resident in another state, but even so, the judges he had put on the bench were known as Bremen's Bums, so maybe it wasn't odd that Teufel was so damned touchy. But what are you going to do to a man who, however he pleads, is going to be found guilty of murder?

"We plead innocent," Andrew Broom repeated, getting between his client and the judge.

"By reason of insanity?"

"No, Your Honor."

"Just innocent?"

"Yes, Your Honor."

"Good luck, Counselor."

"Thank you, Judge."

Broom had everyone baffled by what he was doing. Innocent? Hogan had led them to the body of little Larry Moss, not really buried, just covered with last autumn's leaves and other debris. Cleary had looked up from the grisly sight, but now that they had found the body, Hogan had lost interest and was staring out at the Wabash as if they had marched him out there in handcuffs for a look at the river. The next day Andrew Broom took the case.

"Because he's innocent," Broom answered when Sheriff Cleary asked him why.

"You get him off, Andrew, and people will not appreciate it."

"It is Yoder's job to prove Hogan guilty. He won't be able to."

"Hogan confessed!" Cleary said.

"It won't be admitted in court."

After the way Hogan acted at the preliminary hearing, it was pretty obvious Broom wouldn't be able to put his client on the stand. Hogan would say out loud again that he was guilty, and with the jury listening. He would tell them he had killed Larry Moss and they ought to string him up for it.

"That's a Roger Miller song, Cleary. 'Dang Me.' You should know it."

"Does Hogan?"

"He is a great fan of country-and-western."

Andrew Broom, big shot, Cleary thought. Well, this time he was going to skin his nose and the sheriff for one would be happy to see it. Here he was tonight, postponing his supper so Broom could come and have a talk with Duff Hogan.

Broom brought along his new wife, Susannah. Around the courthouse they were divided between the old wife and the new, but Cleary thought Broom had been lucky twice.

"He's always lucky," Landers said in his whiny voice. "He was born lucky."

"He was lucky his first wife didn't kill him."

"Mine did."

"I thought there was a funny smell in here."

"I could lodge a complaint," Landers whined.

"Against Duff Hogan?"

"Hogan!"

"For sexual harassment."

Landers was so mad he ran short of air before he got out a full sentence, and Cleary let it go. The truth was that Landers *could* bring a complaint against him and probably be successful—that's the way things were going.

Over in St. Joe County, the sheriff was equally worried about his prisoners and his deputies, one of whom, a broad-assed widow whose husband had been a cop, brought charges of sexual harassment against the sheriff. The basis for the charge was that he had told her she would be safe in the Navy when she complained about the toilet facilities. The poor sonofabitch had spent an afternoon before a board with two females on it trying to explain the joke and his chances of reelection were about on a par with Duff Hogan's being found innocent.

"Thanks for letting me see my client at this hour, Sheriff."

"We never close."

"You want rubber gloves, we got 'em," Landers said with a snicker.

Landers should have shut up. Broom asked for two pairs—one for himself, the other for his wife. They would never see those again.

"You owe the county two pairs of rubber gloves," Cleary told Landers when he had put Broom and his wife and Duff Hogan in the consulting room.

"She's better-looking than the first one," Landers said.

He meant Susannah Broom. Maybe he was right. But Dorothy had been a real dish. That didn't change just because she and her boyfriend had tried to get rid of Broom.

SIX

A CAR WAS COMING out his driveway, so Hal Stanfield waited in the street before turning in. Pauline? But the woman behind the wheel of the Mercedes was Silvia Wood. If she noticed him, she gave no sign, but then she was looking into the setting sun when she glanced his way before wheeling into the street and heading like a bat out of hell toward town. Better that than honking her horn and giving him a big hello. Hal just stayed where he was, his mind idling like the motor of his car.

Silvia. Silvia and Pauline. What the hell did that mean? He felt vaguely oppressed, put upon, under attack from every direction. It was an unaccustomed feeling, and he did not like it. The worst reversal had been Andrew Broom. Hal had always considered the man a friend, but in any case he was a man, so why the hell would he take the wife's side in a divorce suit, particularly when the husband was already his client?

Well, he'd meant what he said to Broom. He and Pauline were not going to break up. They would just go on the way they always had. Pauline had no real complaints and, if she did, well, he would give her a longer leash. She bitched a lot that they didn't travel, but whenever he took her along on a trip, she was a pain in the ass, always bored, complaining that all he did was go to meetings.

"It's the point of a convention, Pauline."

"You said we'd go out."

"We will. Tonight's the banquet."

"The banquet!"

"I'm getting an award."

No point in expecting her to be impressed by that. He told her to go shopping, but instead she went to the Museum of Science and Industry and had the time of her life with Corbett, a man from Shipshewana who represented some of the same companies Hal did and who had been a bit surprised to be asked to squire her around.

"Your wife?"

"She's bored."

Corbett, who had the reputation of being a real ass hound, was embarrassed and could not look Hal in the eye. "I don't know, Stanfield."

"I'll do the same for you some day."

Remembering his own overweight, pouty wife, Corbett cheered up and agreed to show Pauline Chicago. The choice of the Museum of Science and Industry mystified Hal, but Pauline had loved it. Well, Corbett was the kind of guy whose charm lasted maybe three days. The second day they went to the planetarium. There wasn't a third day, and probably a good thing. Mrs. Corbett put her foot down and that was that.

Turning into his driveway, he tried to think of Silvia as sort of like Corbett, a way to keep Pauline quiet, but whenever Pauline spent time with Silvia Wood, she was worse. They must sit around talking it up, Pauline saying what a bastard she was married to and Silvia—what would Silvia say? The possibilities did not put Hal Stanfield's mind at rest.

He could see Pauline flaked out on the side porch when he drove by. Probably spent the afternoon out there, drinking with Silvia. If she had a snootful, this was going to be some night.

"You're home early," Pauline said when he came onto the porch and took a chair. She wasn't being sarcastic. Maybe she wasn't sure what time it was.

"I've been golfing."

"Who with?"

"Andrew Broom and his nephew."

"Did he tell you?"

She spoke very deliberately, because she was drunk and did not want to slur her words. Hal felt once more the calm that had come over him in Andrew Broom's office.

"Yes, he told me. I've been thinking about it ever since."

"I've made up my mind."

"I try to imagine what it would be like without you, living alone in this house—"

"Not in this house."

"What do you mean?"

"This house is mine."

That is when the calmness left him. Her house? She must be crazy. What the hell would she do alone in a house like this? She couldn't keep it up on her best day, and her best days were far behind her now.

It might have been righteous indignation that he felt, the champion of home and marriage, but the prospect of Gerald Rowan and Andrew Broom looking into his books at this particular moment was one he could not face. He had never really recovered from Black Monday last October, and too many of the wild cards he had played were turning up losers. He was into silver and gold, for God's sake, he had real money tied up in yen and only an idiot would play the Tokyo market after what Wall Street had done to him. Because he had used a no-load broker on the way up, he had no one to blame but himself, not that he thought he would have done any better with one of the traditional houses. Hog bellies and corn futures had promised to pull him out of it, but they had damned near buried him. One of the ironies of the situation was that the couple of thousand he had put into Silvia's hairdressing and tanning parlors was the best investment he had made all year.

"Why don't you introduce massage?"

"What do you mean?"

"The word new to you or what? Massage. Rubdown. Every city you go to, the yellow pages are full of them."

"Sure, because they're run by Japs and Koreans who'll walk barefoot over your body. I am running respectable places."

"What goes on in the tanning rooms?"

"Everything comes off and that's it. People get a tan. As advertised."

Silvia protested, but Hal had the sense that she was receptive to the idea. He should have done a little research before bringing it up.

"Research it, Silvia, so we know what we're talking about."

"I always know what I'm talking about."

Her jaw came out. He had never met anyone like her. Going to bed with Silvia was like winning a fight. In the sack, she was a spoon, backing up to him, and the trick was to get her on her back. Hal liked the challenge. Also it was a silent bout. Only afterward, half human at last, Silvia liked to lie on her back, one hand on him, the other on her forehead, as if fending off the light.

"There's no more expansion possible in Wyler, Hal."

"You got the place in Privett."

"A mistake."

"Why?"

"I can't keep a close enough eye on it. The manager is stealing, but it would be too much trouble to pin it on her. I don't like anyone stealing from me."

"Massage would mean a whole new clientele."

"And the police."

"The Singapore SinGalore," Hal said, contempt in his voice. The idiot from Chicago who opened that place out on Route 40 might just as well have called it a whorehouse. It was only a matter of time before it was closed down. The guy had tried to get to Cleary, but the sheriff played dumb. Every sheriff in Indiana knew enough to keep Chicago out of his county. Cleary staged a raid, using a deputy named Landers, and it went to court and livened the pages of the *Wyler Dealer* for three weeks while a lawyer from Chicago argued that every war the country ever fought, from the Revolutionary to the Grenada incursion, had as its principal purpose the safeguarding of massage parlors. The prosecutor paraded a procession of Madame Butterflies to the stand, the courtroom was packed, and when it was over fines were assessed and the Singapore SinGalore was shut down.

"You think it could be done right?"

"I think it should be thought about."

Round Two began, thanks to her fidgety hand, and with it silence resumed. Hal did not like the feeling that he was just an instrument Silvia was using, but then he didn't really dislike it either. For a few minutes at least, he was able to forget business, the condition of his finances, and the fact that lots of what was Pauline's alone and in no way theirs was collateral for loans he had no present prospect of being able to pay off.

"What do you and Pauline talk about?"

"Not you."

"You better not."

"Don't worry about me, Hal."

The funny thing is, he never did.

Which is why, having it out with Pauline on the side porch, telling her that there most emphatically would not be any goddam divorce, the thought crossed his inflamed mind that he might ask Silvia to talk sense into his wife's head.

Pauline was out of control now, unloading all the years of resentment on him, her face contorted, her eyes bulging with rage. She was so mad it was almost impersonal. What a shrew she was. He felt like pushing her in the face, knocking her down on the couch, doing her physical harm, and yet the point of this stupid argument was to tell Pauline they were going to stay married whether she liked it or not.

"Till death do us part, remember that?"

"No one would hold me to a promise like that."

Pauline was a bitch. She was cruel to waitresses at the club, to caddies, to attendants at the tennis courts. If these were still the days of servants, she couldn't have kept one for a week. In fact, she was lucky to have a cleaning lady. If his finances were in order, Hal would have dropped her in a minute. She couldn't have been any more fed up with him than he was with her.

The minute things started going right for him again moneywise, Pauline would be out on her ass. It was a promise he was making himself. Meantime, he had to cool this divorce talk. Maybe he would ask Silvia to talk to Pauline.

SEVEN

WHAT GOT SILVIA about Pauline is that she didn't know what a good deal she had. So what if she and Hal were no longer lovers except in a routine sense—that was no reason to make a federal case out of it. She had money of her own, okay, why not use his and hang on to hers and anyway, what did she think awaited her in the wide world at forty-one?

Forty-one! Silvia was thirty-six, claimed to be thirty-two, and thought forty-one was over the hill and no mistake. Pauline really imagined that she could get on a plane and fly into what compared to Wyler would be heaven. Well, Silvia had done what she could to puncture that dream, but then she had trouble imagining what Pauline's present life was like. To her, it had something of the mythic quality Acapulco had for Pauline.

Living with a man. Silvia had been married twice and did not know what it was like to live with a man, day after day, routine, man and wife. Talking with Hal after they made love, isn't that what it was like? She thought of having someone she could say anything to, confide everything, no fear, no holding back. She was a long way from that with Hal, but there were moments when they lay in bed, side by side, that the lovemaking seemed part of something more, not the point of it all, with him getting up and going off to his real life.

He said Pauline turned deaf if he mentioned business and in a way the two of them, she and Hal, talked business, but not the way she would like. They would make a pair, they would. He had seen the potential in the hair-dressing and tanning parlors when banker after banker had looked at her in disbelief. The reception was different after Hal took her side.

They got together the first time in the Roundball Lounge and he said he had heard about her loan applications and would she tell him more.

"I want a loan, not a partner."

"I understand that. But what you may be looking at just now is neither. No bank in Wyler will give you what you want, and I don't need to tell you that if you take your proposal to Chicago, Indianapolis, a city, you got even less of a chance."

He wasn't taunting her, just laying it out, and what he said was what she had come to believe. Her plan pretty well depended on opening three places more or less simultaneously, since she was certain there would be quick competition once the idea caught on. She could start one place and make a success of it and that would soften up the bankers, but maybe for someone else, or someone else with money of their own could come in and undercut her. Silvia had driven to South Bend to take night business courses at IUSB for two solid years, and she had a business plan from which she did not want to deviate. Even so, against all the odds, if it came to that, she would open one place and hope for the best. Hal Stanfield couldn't tell her anything she didn't already know.

She let him buy her a glass of wine and he had a scotch and water, and somewhere about fifteen minutes into the conversation she no longer had the feeling she had when talking with bankers: she knew she was talking to a man. His mouth was weak, but his eyes were cold and she liked that. A big spoiled kid, maybe, but one who was handling Wyler the way he once must have handled his parents. And his interest in her was not just business. It added zest to the conversation, and why the hell not? It wasn't her way to sit on a fortune and not use it. The boy-girl thing was something she understood better than business, and if that is the way her plan could be put into effect, okay.

She got the loan and he was her partner, and she came to know Pauline as a customer first and then a friend and Hal wasn't sure what he thought of that. It was a little confusing for Silvia herself after a while, getting confidences from both of them, not telling the one what the other had said. Maybe it was only natural that she saw Pauline as the problem with the marriage. Talk about spoiled. Pauline had never worked a day in her life, not real work, where she needed the money. All day long she played games—golf, tennis, bridge—or had lunch and got a little tipsy, and at night they dined at one club or another or with friends. And all Pauline did was bitch.

Silvia encouraged her. But not obviously—she didn't want to be accused of deliberately breaking up the Stanfields' marriage.

Her business plan was on track, thanks to Hal.

And now she had another plan. She planned to be the second Mrs. Hal Stanfield when Pauline had gone off to Acapulco or the Canary Islands or wherever.

EIGHT

BEHIND THE BAR at the country club Barany wore a red jacket that had a binding effect on his armpits, but Harrison the manager insisted on it and Barany did not want trouble. What he had wanted was a job where he could keep an eye on Pauline Stanfield without her even knowing he existed.

He had not told Harrison of his education, inventing a fake life to account for the years since high school, claiming to have attended bartender school in Florida. Did Harrison want proof?

Harrison had a turkey neck, a beak of a nose, and narrow little shoulders normally concealed under a jacket, but in his office with only a shirt on they sloped away from his skinny neck for a few inches and that was it. After a moment's hesitation, Harrison gave a little shake of his head.

"You don't need a degree to tend bar."

"It's just a certificate."

Harrison found his range through one of the lenses in his glasses and Barany managed to keep his mouth shut.

"You live in Privett?"

Barany just nodded. Harrison rubbed him the wrong way. Lately, lots of people rubbed him the wrong way. But he had to take them one at a time, and Mrs. Stanfield was first in line.

He had enough on her as it was, but he intended to be fair. The way she had reacted to his telephone pitch was more than enough, but maybe if he knew her better he would change his mind. Crap. What he was betting on was that knowing her better would make him surer she belonged with his parents and Slattery under the concrete floor of the sheet-metal shed in the backyard of the house on the Wabash Road.

The waitresses came to the bar for the drinks and carried them to the tables. Not many people sat at the bar itself, except in the late afternoon and very late at night, mostly men, so what Barany had was an ideal observation post from which he could watch the little tables in the lounge and a good section of the dining room as well.

Pauline Stanfield turned out to be even worse than he had thought. It wasn't because of the drinking; it could be argued that she became less inhuman when she drank, but drunk or sober she was a bitch. Even if he hadn't been an eyewitness, Barany would have been able to keep tabs on her from what the waitresses said.

Noreen the queen, blond and patrician-looking, easily the most popular waitress at the club, very much in command, could be reduced to lip-trembling incompetence by Mrs. Stanfield. It was a campaign that varied from occasion to occasion, so Noreen couldn't get used to it and rise above it. Mrs. Stanfield's contemptuous treatment, not knowing when she would say something unforgivable aloud, unnerved Noreen until she almost longed for the attack to start. Sending back drinks was one way it started; sometimes it was postponed until Mrs. Stanfield questioned the tab she was supposed to sign. The club was a world without money, of course, everything transacted by signature. Ninety-five percent of the tips were add-ons to the bill, so there wasn't the usual controversy about those. Harrison toted them up, divided them equally, and doled them out as if they were his personal largess, as if they made up for the lousy salaries. Ill paid as they were, jobs at the Wyler Country Club were desirable in the local economy; there was even a certain pride felt by the peons at the club, as if some of the social panache rubbed off on them. Barany would have bet Noreen had stuck it out for eight years only because she felt she was almost a member. Maybe it was the independent air she had that brought the vindictive wrath of Pauline Stanfield down on her head.

"Let someone else wait on her," Barany advised.

"She demands that I wait on her. It doesn't matter where my station is."

"Complain to Harrison."

She gave him a look. She was beautiful. He told himself that even if he didn't have his own grievance, Mrs. Stanfield's treatment of Noreen would have decided him. He got so he enjoyed receiving confirmation of the judgment he had made on the basis of that telephone call. He stopped commiserating with Noreen. He never alluded to Mrs. Stanfield. He stood behind his bar and mixed drinks, rearranged glasses and bottles, kept a poker face, and thought about Mrs. Stanfield the way Raskolnikov had thought about the pawnbroker.

He permitted a small smile to dimple the corners of his mouth. How many in the club would even understand the allusion? The thought that he might be the most highly educated person there added to his amusement. Doctors and lawyers were educated only in a sense, and of course there were no professors among the membership of the club for the simple reason that there were no professors in Wyler.

Professors. The little smile went away. Maybe someday he would be able to accept that all those years of graduate study had gone for naught. Even now, unbidden, the hope rose within him that he would go back, register, eat humble pie, and try again. In the early hours of the morning, unable to sleep, he could imagine that return and that triumph. No hard feelings, handshakes all around afterward, the avenue open to a teaching position. Make it a small college, make it a branch of a state university—he would settle for IUSB, if it came to that. Professor Barany. His father had taunted him with that title, treating his defeat as a well-deserved if belated comeuppance. Well, he could rest in peace under that concrete floor, the sonofabitch. His father had hated the Devere in him, had wanted him to fail as if that would give him one more triumph over his ghostly in-laws.

His education was something he must not flaunt at the club; he must give no hint of it. No more than he could let on that he even knew who Mrs. Pauline Stanfield was. He knew a great deal more about her now. That phone call had been pure accident—he was calling randomly selected numbers. For all he knew, she seldom answered the phone herself. It might so easily not have happened. Or so he would have thought until he looked into her background. Her maiden name had been Fortas, which was neither here not there, but her mother had been a Halton!

He couldn't believe it, but there it was in black and white in the *Wyler Dealer*. It was predestined. Vengeance is mine. Pauline Stanfield's Grandfather Halton had been the banker who foreclosed on the Deveres in the Great Depression. She had been a doomed woman before he found out, but now it was only a matter of time. A matter of place. A matter of method.

That was how things stood when the Stanfields showed up at the club that August night. She looked drunk and he looked mad as hell and they wanted to eat. No, they hadn't made a reservation.

Gloria, the hostess, holding the big menu before her like a shield, looked over her crowded dining room. Neither Stanfield liked being told there would be a delay, but then Mrs. Stanfield turned, saw tables in the lounge, and swept toward one in the dimmest corner.

Stanfield tried unsuccessfully to grab her hand when she started off and then stood watching with open disgust as she maneuvered unsteadily across the floor. The only negative aspect of what Barany was going to do to Pauline Stanfield was that it would be a favor to her husband. Stanfield, deciding against a scene, joined his wife in the darkness of the lounge. Barany waited for them to realize that all the waitresses were working the unusually busy dining room.

"Bartender!" Mrs. Stanfield said in a sharp, carrying voice. "Bartender, come here."

It was the first time since the phone call that he had heard that voice, though it had been sounding in his head for months. Because he couldn't see her back in the corner, the voice was a disembodied presence. He could see Stanfield, who turned and made a negative gesture.

"Bartender!"

Barany did not move. Let them have it out together. By the sound of it, she was trying to get to her feet. Maybe the only way her husband could have stopped her was by main force. In the end, they both came to the bar.

"Are you deaf?" she demanded of Barany.

He kept his eyes on the husband. Stanfield shook his head very slightly from side to side.

"Make us up a couple Bloody Marys," he said.

Meaning Virgin Marys, by the look in his eyes. Barany nodded. To hell with him. He ordered Bloody Marys; Bloody Marys he was going to get. He poured generous amounts of vodka over ice and behind him Stanfield cleared his throat significantly. Barany turned.

"I'll bring them to your table."

"We'll have them here," she said contemptuously.

"Let's sit down. I'm tired."

"Well, I'm not. Spend all day on the golf course and come home and say you're tired." She looked at Barany. "Is Andrew Broom in the club?"

"I don't know."

"You don't know what?"

"Pauline, cut it out."

"I won't be talked to like that."

"Let's sit down." He spoke quietly through clenched teeth.

"All right." She plunked down on a bar stood, but not quite solidly. She began to slide off, and a wild look came into her eye. Her husband saved her from an ignominious fall.

"Let's get the hell home," he said. "You're drunk."

She took her drink and threw its contents at him. It hit him in the face and on the shirt front, and ice cubes clattered on the bar and bounced to the floor.

"You lousy bitch!"

Stanfield drew back his arm and was about to give her a punch right in the face, but Barany leaned over the bar and grabbed his arm. It brought his face within inches of Stanfield's, and there was murderous hatred in the man's eyes. His wife got off her stool, but Stanfield saw it. He hit her with his free hand, a long looping slap that sent her staggering across the lounge. She took three tables with her as she went. Even with the carpet it made a hell of a noise.

The dining room emptied. Stanfield was wrestled to the floor. Some women went to help Pauline, but she continued to howl.

"He hit me! You're all witnesses. He hit me!"

Among those who had come from the dining room to see what it was all about was Noreen. Her eyes were wide with wondrous delight as she looked at her disheveled shouting tormentor.

NINE

DUFF HOGAN looked like a beachball and gave the impression of rolling into the room. Landers waited in the doorway as if verifying that the prisoner was now with counsel, then closed the door.

"You know Mrs. Broom," Andrew said, indicating Susannah, who sat off to one side, a pad open on her knee. She smiled at Duff, who ducked his head.

"Are you being treated all right, Duff?" Susannah asked.

A nod of the head.

"Duff, the trial begins tomorrow," Andrew said. "I want to review some things with you now, just a few details. But I have to tell you that things do not look good."

"I did it."

"Did what, Duff?"

"I killed that kid."

"You say you did. The sheriff says you did, and he has had help from the state lab. The prosecutor says you did. Even the *Wyler Dealer* says you did. But I know you didn't."

"I appreciate what you're doing, Mr. Broom."

"What am I doing?"

"Trying to make a jury believe I didn't do it."

"Why would I do that? Duff, if I thought you killed that boy, you could spend the rest of your life in prison and not only would I not care, I'd be glad you were there. Whoever did it ought to pay for it, don't you agree?"

"That's what I'm saying."

"Are you? Then I want a little cooperation so the wrong person doesn't end up in prison. Who did it, Duff?"

Duff let out a prolonged sigh, and Andrew Broom half expected him to deflate as a result of the loss of air.

"Let's review what we know, Duff."

What they knew was that the body of Larry Moss had been found covered with debris near the Wabash River. The sheriff had been led to the body by Duff Hogan, who had come to his office to confess to the crime. No one knew a crime had been committed when Duff confessed to it, saying he had molested and killed a boy by the river. He didn't say who the boy was. He was vague on where he had met Larry Moss, but insisted that he had molested and killed him. The boy was dead enough, but there was no clinical evidence that he had been molested. Sheriff Cleary, with the help of psychiatrists from Indianapolis, had a definition of molestation that was other than clinically testable.

"Molestatio interrupta?" Gerald had asked, and silence fell. Gerald's father had been a professor of classics. No one else knew what the hell he was talking about. He looked around, his smile fading. "Like *coitus interruptus?* The sin of Onan."

"It's not clinically discernible," Cleary went on.

"Were Duff's clothes sent to Indianapolis?" Andrew Broom asked, following Gerald's point.

The sheriff nodded.

"And?"

"Nothing. He says he changed clothes before turning himself in."

But Duff had said that only after the sheriff's questions indicated his clothing did not bear out his confession. If Andrew Broom had ever doubted the wisdom of volunteering to defend Duff, he no longer did. Up to that point he had been relying on what Susannah was perfectly willing to call her woman's intuition.

"Plus the fact that I have known the Hogans all my life," she added. "No member of the Hogan family could possibly do such a thing."

Andrew and Susannah visited the Hogans. They lived on the east side of Wyler, where the town just sort of petered out into open stretches of land, some of it state-owned, purchased when the senator from the district had won the consent of his legislative colleagues to the idea of a park along the Wabash. The land was bought, but in the next election the senator and his party were turned out of office and the land had lain fallow ever since. One result was that the growth of the town had gone in other directions. The street the Hogans lived on reminded Andrew of what the town had looked like just after World War II. The house was a two-story frame whose garage was a barn. The driveway went by the house to the barn, and there was a tank of propane gas mounted on a rusty frame just beyond a pump disconnected from the windmill whose blades creaked in the wind off the river.

Duff got his shape from his mother, that was clear. She was rotund and worried and welcoming, and they went into a kitchen filled with the smell of oatmeal cookies. A tin of them was cooling and several dozen as yet unbaked cookies were arranged on wax paper on a sideboard. Andrew accepted coffee and would have asked for a cookie if Mrs. Hogan had not offered one. At that moment he felt he would betray his country for an oatmeal cookie. In a corner of the room, on a shelf, was a statue of the Virgin with a vigil light burning before it.

When Duff's father came in, a lean man, bald, with a bony nose, he held out a hand that was as long as his forearm.

"I appreciate what you're doing for the boy, Mr. Broom. He didn't kill anybody."

"Why would he say he did it if he didn't?"

They were completely mystified by that and did not try to conceal it. Duff was a good boy, he was religious; for years they had even thought he had a vocation, but it hadn't worked out.

"Barker wouldn't give him a letter."

"Father Barker," Mrs. Hogan corrected. "Our pastor at St. Luke's."

Andrew knew him. He had married Susannah in St. Luke's, not objecting to the priest's officiating as long as she understood he had no intention of becoming a Catholic. He told Barker the same thing.

"No need for that. You're a Christian, aren't you?" Barker's smile seemed an advertisement for denture adhesive. the smile was his permanent expression. He could talk while smiling.

"What does he do at funerals?" Andrew asked Susannah.

"I wish you could have known Father Horvath."

"I knew Horvath." Every Protestant in town had known Horvath, with his Roman collar and dignified air. He was a priest who seemed a worthy opponent.

"He was a more, well, typical priest than Father Barker."

Father Barker felt that all men of goodwill were on their way to heaven—Catholics, Mormons, Jews, and Moslems—who was he to tell God who was who? Andrew thought that God had had something to say on the matter, but he let it go. He had the uneasy feeling that, despite all the disclaimers, Barker was trying to sell something. He was. He was selling Barker, the sinner's friend. Andrew Broom concluded that he didn't want any priest or minister telling him he was all right just the way he was. For that matter, he preferred priests who looked like priests. Barker wore turtlenecks and corduroy jackets and cowboy boots.

Susannah said, "It's ecumenism.

"Is that what it is?"

Gerald overhead this, the conversation having continued in the office, and began to hum. "Winter is ecumenism," he sang aloud. "My father's pun."

"I'll kick your puns," Andrew warned. But he didn't mind Gerald being intelligent in the office. He just had to watch himself in court, where Teufel had a way of punishing intelligence. Anything like erudition enraged the judge.

The realization that the Hogans were Catholic and the mention of Barker sent Andrew to St. Luke's rectory to ask the pastor if he would testify to the good character of Duff.

"How do you mean, his good character?"

"You know what he is going to be tried for?"

"I read the papers."

The thing to watch with Barker was not the relentless smile, but his eyes. It was as if a see-through lens had dropped when he was asked about Duff Hogan.

"The Hogans are parishioners of yours, aren't they?"

"They have been attending St. Luke's since long before I came here."

"How long have you been here, Father?"

Barker wanted to be called Jim, which is why Andrew called him Father. Call no priest Jim, as the Scriptures say. Barker had been pastor of St. Luke's for seven years.

"The Hogans told me Duff had thought of becoming a priest."

"He's not the type."

"How so?"

Barker rolled onto one ham and looked out the window of his office. It was a very neat office. Oddly for Wyler, where there was a black population of maybe a dozen, there was a photograph of Martin Luther King on the wall.

"The Catholic Church has changed since the Council, Andrew. Many Catholics have found that hard to accept. They refuse to be open to change, to move with the Church. In part it is nostalgia, I guess. Time will take care of that. But someone as inflexible as Duff just wouldn't fit into the seminary nowadays."

"How do you mean 'inflexible'?"

The smile became a little pained and the pastoral eyebrows rose to a point above the pastoral nose. "The Hogans have complained about me to the bishop."

"Oh?"

"About the liturgy, about my homilies. About general absolution."

"What's that?"

"In individual confession, the priest gives the penitent absolution for his sins. I prefer a penance ceremony in the church after which I give the congregation absolution as a group."

"Like before going into battle?"

"Exactly!" The smile was radiant again.

"Have you visited Duff in jail, Father?"

He hadn't. Andrew asked the priest if he would.

Now he asked his client, "Did Father Barker come see you yet, Duff?"

"Yes."

"I told him you wanted to go to confession."

Duff just looked at him. Susannah cleared her throat and crossed her legs. Andrew ignored the warning.

"Did you, Duff?"

"He didn't want to hear my confession, but he couldn't refuse."

"You confessed your sins?"

"Andrew," Susannah said pleadingly.

But Andrew had what he wanted. In the crunch, and only in the crunch, he would play the Catholic card. The Mosses had been Catholics too, although Barker had been little more enthusiastic about them than he had been about the Hogans.

"You shouldn't have asked Duff that," Susannah said in the car.

"I didn't ask him what he confessed."

"But you were going to, weren't you?"

He squeezed her hand. "Not with a lady in the room."

They went on to the club and got there in time to see Hal Stanfield strike his wife and send her staggering across the lounge.

TEN

THE COUNTRY CLUB was closer to Privett than to Wyler, but most of the members lived in Wyler. Maybe that is why Barany considered it no hardship to walk from the club to Wyler, going overland as much as he could. Of course, it helped that the Stanfield home was on this side of town.

He was in Phase Three of the project when he began these nighttime reconnaissance missions. He thought of them that way, as paramilitary operations. He wore a navy blue jogging suit, dark tennis shoes, a dark knit cap. The collar of the turtleneck when rolled up came just below his eyes; the cap was pulled down to his eyebrows. He felt invisible flitting over the fields and, when he reached the outskirts of Wyler, falling to a jog.

In Wyler as everywhere now, joggers were a familiar sight, early in the morning, any time of day, late at night. A woman jogger had been brushed by a car at one in the morning in Wyler and the *Dealer* blamed the driver despite his protestations that the woman had been running in the street and was all but invisible because of her dark clothing. The jogger was the underdog. Barany believed the driver and that is how he learned it would be easy to study the object of his intentions in her native habitat.

They went to bed early, he found that out, and at first was disappointed. He had imagined himself observing them through the windows, feeding his hatred with the sight of her in that luxurious home, but the first night he went there after his shift at the country club was over, the house was dark. Perhaps they had not come directly home from the club. But there were three cars in the garage and the hood of one was still warm. The side door of the garage had been left unlocked, so there was no problem gaining entry. He almost regretted that. He wanted to test the skills that were still theoretical, untried. The house proved to be no more difficult.

The doors were locked, even the door of the screened porch. He had continued to circle the house. On the side opposite the porch, balancing it, as it were, was a greenhouse. A side window was angled open and there was no problem getting through it. The floor of the greenhouse was several feet below the house level and a little flight of steps led up to a door. It was unlocked. Barany let himself into the Stanfield home.

The first time, he acquainted himself thoroughly with the ground floor and the basement. It had been a moonlit night and he moved about in the semi-darkness easily. The house was air-conditioned and from time to time the unit in the basement turned itself on. He became attuned to the rhythm of the house. A clock in the living room sounded on the quarter hour, the refrigerator hummed, the little digital clock in the VCR glowed greenly. It was easy, too easy.

The next time, the window in the greenhouse was pulled tightly closed. Why? Had they noticed something that told them he had been inside? He circled the house to check the other doors, and when he was trying the back door, a dog began to growl not six feet from him. Barany's hair lifted from his head and his body was electrified with fear. A dark menacing shape on the lawn, the dog seemed poised to spring, but the Godawful growling grew louder and turned into barking. Barany's cool was completely gone and he was rooted where he stood. He was sure that any movement would cause the dog to attack. It didn't matter. He wouldn't have been able to move.

A window upstairs went up and there was a sound of someone fiddling with the aluminum screen.

"I'll get you, you sonofabitch!"

It was Stanfield's voice. Barany had one hand on the knob of the back door. He looked up, but all he saw was overhang. How the hell could Stanfield see him?

There was the sound of a shot, then another—*pfff*ing, popping percussions. The dog yelped and Barany heard a cocking sound. An air gun? Two more shots and the dog ran whining into the night.

"I got him!" Stanfield crowed. "I got the barking bastard."

There was the muffled sound of Mrs. Stanfield, but then the window was shut.

Barany did not move for three minutes and then he sidled along the house, crossed the yard, and on the side street began to jog, lifting his knees high, tucking in his elbows, looking up at the night sky. At that moment he did not think he would ever return to the Stanfield house.

The sight of her at the club the following afternoon replaced fear with hatred. But cool hatred. He was unobtrusive as always, not wanting to draw attention to himself, but he followed her every movement while she was in sight. In the high court of his mind he had condemned her to death, and the sentence would be executed when and as he pleased.

After the open fight between the Stanfields, when he had stormed from the club and she had been taken away by the Brooms, Barany learned from Noreen that Mrs. Stanfield was going to bring a divorce action against her husband.

"Not because of tonight."

She lifted her eyes. "Of course not. One of my tables was talking about it."

"She's divorcing him? I thought she was the one fooling around."

"They both were."

"How do you know that?"

She put two long lovely fingers behind the shell of her ear. "We hear a lot in the dining room."

"What you hear at a bar you tend to discount."

"Take my word for it. And gimme two brandies and a bourbon on the rocks."

Noreen was divorced herself. That is all Barany knew. Did he want to know more? She treated him like a bartender, what else, with condescension. Sometimes he imagined telling her what he really was, but he did not think hearing about his graduate studies would make her less haughty. If he was so damned smart, why was he tending bar at the country club? Waiting until the money he had inherited could be turned over to him. In his mind's eye, she laughed derisively when he told her that, and her imagined laughter made him feel like a pretender, an impostor. Deposed prince tends bar at country club. Shades of Huckleberry Finn and the Duke and Dauphin! The hell with it. He was not interested in impressing Noreen. Her grammar was unsure, she was shrewd rather than intelligent, her beauty could not overcome her deficiencies.

Or so he told himself, but the sight of her could make him catch his breath and feel a constriction in his chest more binding than the little red jacket he wore behind the bar. He drove the thought away by asking what changes in his plan the Stanfield divorce would make.

None. Why should it? Divorces take time. She wasn't going anyplace. He gave the stainless steel behind the bar a rubdown. Where was Pauline Stanfield now? She had left with the Brooms. Presumably, because of the public brawl, they had taken her home with them.

But when his shift was over, he dialed the number of the Stanfield home and after three rings it was answered by Mrs. Stanfield.

"Mrs. Harold Stanfield?"

"Who is this?"

"Mrs. Stanfield, I'm calling on behalf of Omega Roofing and I want to acquaint you with our late summer offer—"

"Do you know what time it is?"

"It's never too late for an Omega roof, Mrs. Stanfield."

"Spell it!"

"I beg your pardon."

"Something or other roofing. Spell it."

"Spell it? Certainly. I-T."

"You sonofabitch."

"A free inspection of your roof includes checking—"

She hung up with a bang. Barany hung up himself and turned to face Noreen.

"What are you doing, making obscene phone calls?"

"Why do you ask?"

One corner of her mouth went up in a crooked smile. "What were you saying?"

"It's a gag I play on a friend. Got a ride home?"

"I've got a car." She was looking at him as if she did not believe his explanation. How much had she heard? He had used Mrs. Stanfield's name a lot.

"I'm asking, not offering."

"Something wrong with your car?"

"It'll be fixed tomorrow."

"I don't know where you live."

"I do."

She decided that was funny. "All right, let's go. I got to hurry. My daughter's alone until I get there."

He told her to take a left when they went through the gates of the club.

"Left?"

"Yeah. How old's your daughter?"

"Twelve, nearly thirteen. An awful age."

"Pimples?"

"Pimples! She wears the same size bra I do."

Her laugh was husky, almost suggestive, but maybe he was imagining things. She smiled into the oncoming darkness as she drove.

"What's the address?"

"It's on the Wabash Road."

"Where on the Wabash Road?"

"This side of Privett."

She slowed down and turned to him. "Privett!"

"Look, I'm sorry. I can walk, that's okay. Just pull over."

"Walk to Privett? You must be nuts."

So she drove him home, put out but half pleased that she had not taken him up on his offer to let him walk. His car was parked in the lot at the club. He had asked for the ride on an impulse, to be with her, but with unconscious shrewdness too, as if he already knew the moment had arrived.

"What did you do before you started tending bar at the club?" Noreen asked.

"I worked in Minneapolis."

"And you came back to Wyler!"

"Privett."

"That's even worse."

He told her he would get off at the end of the driveway, but she said, "What the heck," and turned in.

"Are you married?"

"No."

"This your house?"

"My parents left it to me."

"No one's home."

"I live alone."

"You have that whole house to yourself?"

A reply to that sprang to his lips, but he repressed it. He suddenly realized that Noreen now saw him as a man of means. Well, he was.

"I'm divorced," she said.

"That's what I heard."

"Who told you?"

"I asked."

"Oh." She leaned over the wheel, looking at the house.

"I'd invite you in—"

"No, no. I've got to get home to my daughter." She smiled at him. "Do you have any kids?"

"I'm not married."

"Never have been?"

"No one ever asked me."

She was still laughing when he got out of the car. He looked in before closing the door.

"Thanks for the ride. I'll do the same for you sometime."

He directed her as she used the turnaround. His was not a road you backed into if you could avoid it, not even at this hour. She gave a little toot on her horn before turning onto Wabash, then goosed the car and sped off into the night.

ELEVEN

SILVIA HAD RENTED a tape of *The Sting* and settled down to a quiet evening of popcorn, beer, ragtime music, and a movie she had already seen a dozen times and liked better every time. Robert Redford, Paul Newman, and Robert Shaw, all in the same film—what more could you ask?

She ate more popcorn than she should, drank three beers, and had just lit up as the film began its final part when Hal called, so excited he didn't make much sense. He'd had a fight with Pauline, that much she got.

"Where are you?"

"Downstairs."

"Downstairs!" She could kick herself for having answered the phone. But at least he was calling from the lobby.

"Can I come up?"

She looked around the living room. It was a mess. One of his complaints about Pauline was that she was a slob, and Silvia knew the complaint was justified. Normally, her own place was spick-and-span, but she had come in exhausted, just thrown things down, wanting to clear her mind of everything and enjoy the movie. Thank God she had opened the windows before lighting up, but even so the room was full of smoke. She nipped the burning end of the joint into an ashtray and put the remainder in the pocket of her robe. Waste not, want not.

"Sure. Come on up."

She was gathering things into her arms as she hung up the phone—the newspaper, her purse, beer cans, and the bowl half full of cold popcorn. When she had gotten rid of those, she came back, fluffed up the pillows on the couch, and picked up a paper napkin. The place looked okay. There was a tap on the door and she let him in.

As soon as she closed the door, he took her by the arms and looked into her eyes. "Silvia, I hit Pauline, in public, in the bar at the club. I knocked her ass over teakettle with God knows how many people looking on."

He seemed to want some special reaction and she didn't know what it was.

"Come in, sit down. Do you want something to drink?"

"What are you having?"

"Well, I had a beer."

"A beer would be fine. What's that smell?"

She looked at him, sniffed a bit. "What do you think?"

"Popcorn?"

God, what a relief. "My secret vice."

"Is there any left?"

"I'll make some more."

He came into the kitchen with her and told her at least three times what had happened at the country club, at each telling making Pauline come off worse and himself better. Meanwhile, her electric popper set off a racket and puffy popped kernels started to cascade into the bowl.

"She had it coming, Silvia."

She shrugged.

"You don't agree."

She poured melted butter over the popcorn and handed him the bowl.

"Napkins over there." She opened the refrigerator and took out two cans of beer. "Want a glass?"

"Can's fine."

They marched into the living room. The television screen was an ectoplasmic blur. Silvia punched a button to rewind the tape.

She turned to Hal, her head a little light from the joint, and felt in charge.

"You want to know what I think?"

He nodded, the can of beer to his lips.

"I'm surprised one or both of you hasn't gotten violent before this."

"I never hit her before. I want you to know that. Not even when she kicked and clawed and threw things."

"She's done that?"

"Does the bear sleep in the woods?"

"But not in public?"

He thought about it. "I guess not. But not because she wouldn't. The occasion just never arose." He took another swallow of beer. "I still cannot believe I belted her in front of all those people."

"What happens now?"

But he was still seeing the scene in his mind. "Maybe if the bartender hadn't grabbed my arm I wouldn't have done it. I don't know."

"That's how both my marriages ended, violently. I was afraid of being killed and even more afraid that I would kill my husband."

"I know what you mean."

"So what are you going to do?"

He thought about it, his eyes darting back and forth as if he were trying to read something, then shook his head. "She wants a divorce."

"Hal, it sounds like you're both ready for one." He looked at her and she wondered if she had made a wrong move. "I mean, based on my own experience."

"We're not getting a divorce."

"You mean you aren't."

"I won't let her divorce me, Silvia. Not now. What the hell difference does it make whether we're divorced or not? It's not as if she wanted to marry someone else."

Silvia put her hand in the pocket of her robe and her fingers closed on the joint. There were matches in the other pocket. She took out the joint and lit it, dragging the smoke in deep and holding it. He watched her do this and his mouth fell open.

"You're smoking."

"It's my place."

"I didn't know you smoked."

"Just these."

"What is it?"

She held out her cupped hand. "Try it."

"Is it marijuana?"

"Haven't you ever tried it?"

"No."

She brought her hand back. "I sure don't want to lead you astray." She took another drag, looking at him as she did.

"Do you have another?"

She held it out again. This time he took it, holding it delicately between thumb and forefinger, bringing it slowly to his lips. He hesitated and then sucked greedily.

Before it was over they had smoked the four others she had hidden in a kitchen canister, smoked them in the bedroom, in bed. Silvia could not believe that a forty-three-year-old man had never smoked pot. It was like discovering he was a virgin. If he had been, they took care of that too.

Afterward, lying on her back beside him, staring at the ceiling, it occurred to Silvia that this was all wrong. This was rebound stuff. A fight with the wife and he came to her and she took him in, a port in the storm. Up until now a little sack time had been all right—they were business partners, after all—but if she aspired to be his wife, she was going about it all wrong. It would have been much wiser to encourage him to say all the awful things about Pauline while seeming to find excuses for her. A tricky thing to do, of course. She didn't want to seem in league with the enemy, but she was certain it had been a big mistake to be such easy consolation for him on this night above all others.

She rolled abruptly out of bed and began to get into her robe.

"Hey," he protested.

"Hal, listen to me." She sat on the edge of the bed, grabbed his wrists when he began to grope, and held them tight.

"Let's have another smoke."

She ignored that. Even if she'd had more, she would have refused. The pot had been another mistake. What had she been thinking of? Getting him into a weakened condition, that's what, and she had succeeded all too well.

"Where is Pauline right now, Hal?"

"I don't give a damn where she is."

"Would she have gone home with the Brooms?"

He made a face. He didn't want to think about it. "What difference does it make?"

"None, if you want her to have the house."

He got up on one elbow. "What do you mean?"

"Think about it, Hal. This is a crucial moment. You have had a public fight with Pauline. Whoever claims the house now gets the house. If she says she is leaving you, she can hardly move back into the house with you."

"She's not leaving me. I told you that."

"It may not be up to you. Particularly if Andrew is her lawyer."

"I don't think she went home with them."

"So she is at your house?"

He nodded. He threw back the sheet and Silvia turned away. But in the mirror she could see that he was dressing.

"You're leaving?"

"I'm going home."

"Where Pauline is?"

"It's my house too."

"She won't let you in."

He laughed. "I'll let myself in."

She turned to him. "I guess I don't understand you, Hal. You come here and tell me for hours what a bitch Pauline is. You hit her in public. That could be interpreted as the big good-bye. She wants a divorce. You say you won't permit it. Now you want to rush off to be in the same house with the woman you hate. I don't get it."

He was slipping his feet into his loafers. "It sounds crazy, Silvia, but it isn't. Believe me, it isn't."

"I have to believe you because I sure as hell don't understand it."

She followed him into the living room. He took a handful of what was left in the popcorn bowl and it seemed to remind him.

"Silvia, I really appreciate this. I do. And what I'm doing does make sense. For now. It does." He hesitated as if he wanted to say more, and then he added, "I can't afford a divorce right now."

"What's to afford?"

But he had said all he was going to. She put her head against the closed door after he was gone and asked herself what she could have done to make it end differently.

Two sleepless hours later she still did not have an answer to that question.

TWELVE

GERALD ROWAN had joined his Uncle Andrew's law firm out of a mixture of motives, some of them professional, some not. Andrew had assured him that, far from specializing in one small corner of the law, he would be involved in the whole legal spectrum though on a smaller stage. Moreover, Gerald could expect to earn a good deal more a good deal sooner working with his uncle than with any of the prestigious Chicago firms that had offered him a job. Andrew's claims had all proved true.

At the time Gerald made his decision, he did not have to take his uncle's word that the golf courses in the Wyler area were superb. He played them. He learned that Andrew, several times state amateur champion, was still an extraordinarily good golfer. The country club course had been laid out by Jack Nicklaus and Walnut Grove by Arnold Palmer. Those courses alone would have decided Gerald, even if practicing law in Wyler had looked like early retirement.

What Uncle Andrew had not mentioned and what would have proved decisive was Julie McGough.

Julie insisted on driving from the men's tees when they golfed together, and even at that it was not easy for Gerald to beat her. A woman with a short but accurate game can easily embarrass a slugger whose three-hundred-yard drives are likely to end up anywhere in the county. But Julie, like Gerald, had a long and powerful game which lost little in accuracy. Most important, she was a competitor. She'd played with her brother Stan for too many years to imagine a man was somehow by nature a better golfer than she. Only once did Gerald, out of misguided gallantry, play below his game. That was the first time they had gone out together, and he had to scramble from the third hole. She beat him only because she had a higher handicap, but she might have beaten him without it. Gerald never again played for anything but blood with Julie.

An odd consequence of this was that on the golf course she was far more susceptible to his charms than off. If a week went by without a match, Gerald found Julie growing aloof. It did not help—indeed things got worse— if he then wooed her in the usual way, plying her with gifts, taking her to diverting concerts, dancing her shoes off. But eighteen holes of cut-throat golf made Julie a clinging malleable female.

Today, despite the fact that he had spent the afternoon at Walnut Grove, they had gone out just before six, and when they reached number sixteen, a favorite hole, Julie was down three and breathing hard, her eyes bright when she looked at Gerald. The green was an island; the tee was on a hill so that one looked down at water and the enisled green. Gerald, with the honors, stroked a wedge shot that sent his ball high in the air on a perfect trajectory. It reached its apex and then fell like a rock, remaining where it landed, two feet from the hole.

"You missed," Julie said.

"Show me how it's done."

She hit a nine iron, not getting the loft she should have, and her ball described a dying arc and looked as if it would be in the water short of the green, but then, as if influenced by her body English, the ball hit the very edge of the island, bounced almost vertically, dropped again, and unaccountably ran toward the hole, stopping about ten feet shy.

"What'd you use, a putter?"

"I will if you don't shut up."

"You should keep your left shoulder under your chin."

"When does your book come out?"

"I was thinking of a video."

They held hands as they went down the precipitous path to the water. To the left, a short fairway where they had left their cart followed the curve of the shore to a bridge by which access to the green could be had, but directly below the green a boat was moored, there for those whose balls went into the water and who wanted to try retrieving them. For Julie and Gerald that boat had become a rendezvous.

The course was deserted now, twilight was at hand. In the still air the surface of the lake was mirror smooth, the long chevrons created by indolent ducks widening like vectors on the water. Gerald helped Julie into the boat, pushed off, and took her in his arms. Her lips hungrily sought his. Thank God for that approach shot. Anything less and her ardor might have cooled.

Some ten feet from shore the boat slowed and stopped and then turned in a lazy circle as they grappled in its ribbed confines. The salty taste of her sweat was an aphrodisiac, her splayed hands on his back sought to negate his otherness and bring them even closer. Meanwhile, his elbow was pinched against the side of the boat and his knee pressed painfully against the seat on which she sat. In a minute they fell free of one another and she breathed heavily against his chest.

"I am christening this boat the *Foreplay*."

Her breathing continued.

"It is more effective than a chastity belt."

"Be grateful for what you have."

"I'll remember that."

Suddenly, she struggled free and sat upright on the seat. "Say," she began.

"Yes."

"You were going to explain to me why your uncle is defending Duff Hogan."

"Do you object to the trial system, a citizen's right to counsel, or what?"

"He's a pervert."

"That's the charge."

"He admits it."

"Andrew doesn't believe him."

"On what grounds?"

"Come to the trial and find out."

Gerald wished he himself understood Andrew's reasons for volunteering to defend Hogan. The little butterball looked weird enough to Gerald to have done what he claimed. The reason seemed to be Susannah, only that wasn't a very good reason. That she couldn't imagine someone she knew doing such a thing was a plus for her rather than for Hogan.

"Oh, it's a bit more than that," Andrew had replied when Gerald offered this theory.

"You have an eyewitness who saw him not do it?"

A small grin was all that got, which was all it deserved.

"It has something to do with his religion," Andrew said.

"He's Catholic."

"Yes."

"A ritual murder?"

"He is innocent, Gerald. He confessed to a crime he knows few details about. He claims to have sexually assaulted the Moss boy, but Duff's knowledge of sex is minimal. There is no evidence on the body nor on Duff that any such molestation occurred."

"Maybe he just killed him."

"That presumably will be Yoder's line when I establish that there is reasonable doubt of any sexual assault. There is still a dead boy. Murdered."

"How?"

"Garroted. A rope twisted around his throat. Which has never been found, of course. Duff's description of the instrument is vague in the extreme. My defense will be that there is reasonable doubt (a) that sexual assault occurred and (b) therefore that a man who claims to have assaulted Larry Moss and then killed him may be presumed to be lying on both counts."

"Why?"

"I am still groping for the best way to put it."

"But it has something to do with religion?"

"How does that go? 'Greater love than this hath no man than he lay down his life for his friends.' He is sacrificing himself."

"For whom?"

"I don't know."

In the boat on the lake at the sixteenth hole, Julie said, "Of course, my father hopes that Andrew Broom will at last make a public fool of himself."

The rivalry between his uncle and Frank McGough was one of the small-town mysteries Gerald despaired of understanding. Andrew and Julie's father had been boys together. They had been vying with one another for primacy since grade school, and each was a resounding success, one in law, the other in banking. Wyler benefited from each man's resolution that the other should not surpass him in making the town prosper. Maybe in their case being enemies was the only way they could be friends. But it sure didn't help when it came to Gerald and Julie.

"I ask nothing else of you but this, Gerald," Andrew had said. "Don't get mixed up with Julie McGough."

"What's wrong with Julie?"

"Her father."

"She can't do much about that."

"That's what I mean. There are lots of other girls."

Not a wholly accurate portrait of Wyler, yet not false either. But prohibition had its usual effect, and Gerald immediately found Julie more attractive than before.

"What has your father got against my uncle?"

"Everything."

"Meaning you don't know."

"It happened before I was born."

"Ah. You are Uncle Andrew's illegitimate child."

"What a thing to say!"

Julie looked more like her father than she did her mother.

"I meant he's your mother."

He liked it when she punched his arm. That gave him a chance to grab her wrist and wrestle her into submission. Maybe she liked whips too.

Light receded and they pulled out, birdie, par, and got into the cart.

"Had enough?"

"There are only two more holes."

What he liked about her was that she didn't give up. He knew she was determined to beat him. Unfortunately, Gerald hooked his drive on seventeen, and while they looked for it, definitive dark descended.

"You hooked on purpose," she accused.

"Of course."

"Bah." They continued up the fairway toward the clubhouse, whose lights twinkled through the trees. "Let's putt on eighteen."

"I can't see."

"It might improve your game," she said.

"How will I know if I can't see?"

"Why don't you become a lawyer when you grow up?"

"I think I love you."

"Don't bother."

"There's an opening if the Stanfields divorce."

"What do you mean?"

"We can get married."

"Not tonight. I have a headache."

On the eighteenth green they putted in the dark and then went inside, where they were told of the fight between the Stanfields.

"Let's have dinner together," Gerald said.

"I'm dining with my parents."

"But I have all sorts of gossip. She wants a divorce."

"That's not news."

"He's my client."

"Hal Stanfield?"

"Just for the divorce. Uncle Andrew's her lawyer."

"Boy, nothing gets out of the firm, does it? But you better check. My father says there's no way in the world the Stanfields are going to get a divorce just now."

"Why would he say that?"

"He didn't say."

A small light, about twenty watts, went on in Gerald's head. McGough was a banker. Hal Stanfield was a regular buccaneer of the business world, his independent insurance agency providing venture capital for his widespread wheeling and dealing. It would be interesting to know if McGough's remark related to Hal Stanfield's business dealings. Well, Gerald would find out soon enough when he and Uncle Andrew sat down and began to develop the terms of an amicable settlement.

THIRTEEN

AFTER SHE DROPPED Barany off at his home on the Wabash Road, Noreen drove back to Wyler in pensive silence. It is a truth universally acknowledged that a single man in possession of a home needs a wife.

Whenever she discussed it with her parents or friends, Noreen insisted that she never intended to marry again, once was more than enough for her; she had Karen and a good job and that was plenty.

"It's Karen I'm thinking of," her mother said. "She needs a father."

"She's got a father."

A father! Harry in his mid-thirties still had the mentality of a teenager. He dressed like a teenager, he hung out with teenagers, he held the job of a teenager, parking cars in Chicago—Harry and the blacks, hoping for tips, looking forward to a big night. What a creep. But what an idiot she had been to marry him a month shy of her eighteenth birthday, Karen already on the way, throwing away any future she had. She was beautiful, she knew that; she had brains. And she was a waitress. In order to be anything else, she would need breaks she wasn't going to get. In her heart of hearts, she knew that the only thing that could bail her out was to marry a grown-up man who would take care of her. That is why she always said she would never marry again.

She had learned not to hope.

She had learned to keep her dreams to herself.

Was Barany the one? On the face of it, the thought was crazy. A bartender? Noreen knew all she needed to know about bartenders. They were only a notch or two above Chicago parking attendants, the main difference being a clean shirt and clean hands.

She had scarcely noticed Barany before tonight. Oh, she had talked with him—she talked with everyone, good old Noreen—but basically Barany was a bartender and she knew what she thought of bartenders. When he asked for a ride tonight, she had been on her guard, figuring that, being a bartender, he would probably make some kind of pass. When he said he lived in Privett, she thought she had been had and she was in a bad mood by the time she got to the Wabash Road. Then, all of a sudden, Barany was a homeowner, a man of means. Unmarried.

So what was he doing tending bar at the country club in Wyler? Why was he unmarried? Tantalizing thoughts, intriguing thoughts. She drove home with them and they stayed with her through the predictable fight with Karen, who held the phone as if she had been on it all night and did not want to go to bed. She mixed a spritzer and put on Paul McCartney and turned the questions over and over in her mind.

Now that she thought about it, Barany didn't talk like a bartender. Why did she say that? It was hard to put her finger on it, but that didn't make her any less certain. Odd that Barany should have been caught up in the Stanfield fight.

Stanfield. Sitting alone in the living room of her cheapo apartment with the paper-thin walls and Karen probably lying in bed with earphones on, listening to music night and day when she wasn't on the phone, Noreen felt any moral authority she should have over her daughter disappear at the thought of Hal Stanfield.

Even before anything happened, even without having been warned of the members with the roving eyes, Hal Stanfield above all, she should have known the first time he looked at her that he was trouble. She could preach a sermon on how stupid it was for a girl to get involved with a married man like Hal Stanfield. There wasn't anything she didn't know about how stupid it was, and yet she had gone ahead.

Not even the thought of the other girls' talk stopped her. She knew what they must be saying because she would have said the same thing about any of them. What a stupid bitch. Any girl over fourteen would know that he was a big spoiled brat interested in no one but himself and whatever fun he could have, whatever the cost to someone else.

So why did she have an affair with Hal Stanfield?

An affair! Even now she tried to dress it up with dignity. Or maybe using that word explained it. It wasn't just a roll in the hay, a shackup—it was an affair. Upward mobility, mixing with the upper classes. She had actually thought he was doing her a favor taking advantage of her. The only crumb of self-respect she could come up with was her refusal ever to bring him to her apartment.

So there had been motels in South Bend and points in between—cheap, cheap, cheap. Every time was to be the last time. She would go with him again only to explain why this could not go on, which was to deal him a very powerful hand since, if this was the last time, well, how about it? She was flattered. She knew she was better-looking than his wife. She knew she was better-looking than Silvia Wood.

Silvia. The worst part of all was thinking of Silvia.
Noreen had spied on Hal. She had acted like a wife.
When his interest waned, rather than be grateful, she had
been insulted. Was he simply being faithful to his wife?
Maybe if she hadn't known what a witch Pauline Stanfield was, Noreen could have believed that and allowed
the thing to fade away. The thought that he was fooling
around with someone else got to her and she had to know
if it was true.

Her cheeks burned at the memory of following him.
Three different times, with her shift hardly begun, she
had claimed illness and left because Hal was leaving and
she wanted to know where he was headed.

The first time he went straight home and that was it.
Noreen circled the block a couple of times, considered
returning to the club to announce her miraculous recov-
ery, but went home herself. The second time he drove to
what she would learn was the building where Silvia Wood
had her apartment. Hal had a key.

Her first thought was that he had never offered her an
apartment, but then she supposed that this girl had been
stupid enough to let him talk his way into using her place
for their get-togethers.

Only Silvia wasn't stupid. Silvia was a business-
woman, and right away Noreen felt that they had lots in
common. Silvia's background was even more humble
than Noreen's, she had had two husbands but no kids,
and she obviously knew how to handle Hal Stanfield. She
got to know Silvia by having her hair done at her shop.

"The country club," Silvia said the first time. She was
keeping the appointment book, but said she would do
Noreen's hair herself. The usual compliments on her hair,
with Silvia telling her she should never touch it up, the
natural color was perfect, and the body! What care did

Noreen give it? With a little tan, Noreen would be a knockout.

"Married?"

"Divorced."

A sigh. "You too?"

"Good riddance."

"How long have you been at the country club?"

"Eight years."

"You must know everyone who belongs."

"I suppose."

"I've never been near the place."

"You could afford to join."

Silvia laughed. "Maybe I will. I know people who belong."

"I would know them."

"The Stanfields?"

"Oh, sure." And Noreen had an awful thought that Hal might have told Silvia of her, but no, not even Hal was that kind of bastard. He wouldn't admit that infidelity was a habit with him. Even now, when she knew about Silvia, he talked as if Noreen was the only lapse in an otherwise perfect marriage. He didn't want to think of himself as a chaser.

"Mrs. Stanfield is a friend of mine."

"A customer?"

"That too."

"Maybe I'll see you as her guest at the club."

She said that, thinking Silvia was inventing the friendship with Mrs. Stanfield, not wanting to say it was Hal she knew, but a week later, there was Silvia at lunch with Pauline Stanfield. Noreen waited to see if Silvia would recognize her. She did, and for a change Pauline Stanfield did not badger her.

Leo Barany, the bartender, noticed Mrs. Stanfield's guest. He looked surprised, as if he knew who Silvia was.

"They have more in common than you'd think," Noreen said, looking at Leo.

She ended up thinking that she and Silvia were friends rather than rivals. Well, they weren't friends, and they had been rivals, and Silvia had won Hal Stanfield, if that was the right word.

FOURTEEN

BARANY WATCHED Noreen's car take off toward Wyler, then went inside the house, lighted at least one lamp in every room, turned the television on full blast, and changed into a black sweater and pants and running shoes. Pulling the wool cap over his head, he took off across the Walnut Grove Golf Course, moving at a steady jog, the rhythmic beat of his tennis shoes on the fairway grass taking the place of thought. Thought came later, after he reached the country club and his car. He eased out of the lot and was soon accelerating up the road to Wyler.

When he called and found Pauline Stanfield at home, he knew the time had come. The plan and timing had been deliberately left flexible, so that he could profit from any unforeseen turn of events. The brawl between the Stanfields at the club had provided that turn.

He could draw a floor plan of her house. He knew he could do this because he had done it. Sometimes at night, lying in the dark, he had pressed his eyes shut and imagined himself moving through the Stanfield home.

No need to bother with the greenhouse window now. One day he had noticed Hal Stanfield pull his key case from his raincoat pocket as he was getting ready to leave the club. The next rainy day, when Stanfield came to the club, Barany went into the cloakroom and removed the keys from his pocket. In a South Bend mall he had duplicates made. The first chance he had, he slipped the key case back into the raincoat pocket. Stanfield had kicked up a fuss over the loss of his keys, but when he pulled them from his pocket, he looked startled, then sheepish. Without a word he put the keys back in his pocket and strode out of the club. It was just a week ago that Barany had admitted himself to the Stanfield house by the back door at three in the morning and spent half an hour acquainting himself with it.

Upstairs he learned that the Stanfields slept in separate rooms, she in the master bedroom at the front of the house that had windows on three sides. There was a bathroom and a dressing room opening off the bedroom. His room was down the hall, a combination den and sleeping room, its sideboard and refrigerator ensuring that Hal Stanfield need never go to bed sober.

Even as he moved through the house, Barany kept an open mind. It would happen as it happened, he told himself. Barany felt he was waiting for the inevitable and had become an instrument of fate.

And now the moment had struck.

Tonight was the night.

He would kill Pauline Stanfield and bury her in the metal shed behind his house on the Wabash Road, under the concrete floor with his parents and Slattery. How would he kill her? He shook his head gently and smiled. Let it happen, he murmured to himself, let it happen.

When he reached Wyler, he took the belt line and entered town on the opposite side from the area in which the Stanfields lived. He had verified that one of the keys he had duplicated was to Silvia Wood's building. The idea had come to him because of something Noreen had said when Silvia was Mrs. Stanfield's guest for lunch, the way she said the two had lots in common. Leo suspected Mr. Stanfield was one of the things they had in common. He was right. Stanfield's car was parked, bold as could be, on the street in front of the building. Barany nodded as if a detail of his plan had fallen into place.

Stanfield was with his mistress. His wife would be alone in the house. That increased Barany's options. There were many ways he could do what he had come to do. He might even take her unconscious but still alive to his house and kill her there. It was possible, he said half aloud, as if conceding a well-argued point.

Having parked on a side street from which the Stanfield yard could be reached, he moved in feline fashion along a line of trees, went sideways through an opening in the hedge probably made by a paperboy, crossed silently over the lawn to the back porch, and eased open the aluminum door.

After he had put the key in the lock, he stood for a moment before turning it. The throb of his heart was audible to his inner ear, he was breathing rapidly. It was a moment to savor, and savor it he did, daring fate, a suspicious figure sandwiched between the open aluminum screen door and the inner as yet unopened door. He turned the key slowly and heard the lock slide free. There was an almost sensuous pleasure to be had from turning the knob 180 degrees and then applying pressure on the door. Then he was inside.

Leaving the door ajar, he stood listening to the sounds of the house. Music. Muted, distant, but music without a doubt. It came from upstairs. There was a lamp lit in the living room, a small lamp on top of a cabinet, with a ribbed rose-colored shade. It might have been a night-light left on for her husband.

Barany mounted the steps two at a time to the landing, where he paused. Sinatra? Some crooner from an earlier time, the kind of music Barany's mother had enjoyed. He snuffed out that thought. He had not willingly thought of his mother for months; it was too painful.

Barany put one foot on the next stair, but before he moved, she began to sing along with Frank, her voice beginning low and then gaining confidence if not quite the tune. *Come fly with me.* There was a sense of shared insouciance in her tone. Like Frank, she would thumb her nose at the world and take her pleasure where she found it. But her voice was as drunken as it was defiant.

Barany reached the upstairs hallway, turned toward the den, and all but ran to it. Once inside the room, he eased himself down on the single bed. He sat there in the dark, on the edge of Stanfield's bed, a smile on his face, listening to a woman who would shortly die singing a song that had been popular a quarter of a century before.

At a time of his own choosing, he would go down the hall and kill her. Strangle her. Yes. The way little Larry Moss had died. Not that he contemplated a sexual assault. The thought of making love to Pauline Stanfield was repellent. Killing her would be more satisfying than sex.

FIFTEEN

WHENEVER HE LEFT SILVIA, Hal Stanfield felt a momentary repentance, and he could imagine that he was going home to his wife for good, turning over a new leaf. Stolen pleasure loomed large in anticipation, but when the night was over, it seemed a minor thing.

Oh, he liked Silvia well enough. She was a good companion in and out of bed; he had no complaint at all. But infidelity was socially disruptive and Stanfield, unembarrassed by the pomposity of the thought, felt he owed something to western civilization, and he meant to pay the debt. Going home to Pauline was about as penitential a thing as he could do.

Of course, this time was different, after what had happened at the club.

It was easy with Silvia to dream of being free of Pauline. Why, he might even marry Silvia and then everything would be all right. An impossible dream, at least for now; he just could not afford it. That is why he was driving at forty-five miles per hour through the dark streets of Wyler, on his way home to the wife he had struck in public only a few hours before. He did not relish the reception he would get, but he would just tough it out. It was better to get it over with.

Funny, he still could not believe he had actually belted Pauline in the club lounge. God knows she had deserved it, but who was going to sympathize with a man who struck a woman? Nobody, that's who. He himself felt more guilt than satisfaction when he thought of Pauline reeling backward into those tables after he had struck her.

As he turned the corner into his street, Stanfield's heart sank. There were lights on in the house, lights on in Pauline's bedroom. He reached forward and doused his headlights, slipping along in the dark, easing into the driveway, letting the car move on idle. He bent over the steering wheel and looked up to see if there was any sign Pauline had heard the car approach. He saw none.

Just beyond the side porch, he brought the car to a slow stop and turned off the motor. The door seemed to set off a racket loud enough to wake the dead as he got out of the car. He pushed the door closed but did not shut it entirely, fearing the sound it would make. He took off his shoes and tiptoed toward the house.

The back door was ajar, and, noticing this, he hesitated. Had she just now come home and burst into the house, taking possession? Carrying his shoes, Hal went inside, closed the door, and locked it.

In stocking feet, he went upstairs and paused in the upper hallway, about to head for his room. But that was nonsense. He turned to the right and entered Pauline's room.

Every light but the ceiling light was on, music oozed from the speakers that stood in opposite corners of the room, the bed had been turned back, and there was a drink on the nightstand. But no Pauline. The bathroom door was closed, and as he approached it, Hal heard the sound of the shower.

Surprise her in the shower? Good God no. He must not frighten her. He retraced his steps, once more on tiptoe, but when he came out of the room, he stopped dead. A man about to start downstairs turned to face Hal. He was dressed all in black, his cap was pulled low over his forehead, and the neck of his sweater covered his mouth. Hal's breath caught and his body prickled with fear. All he could see of the man's face were his eyes. Familiar eyes. The bartender! The bastard who had grabbed his arm when he tried to hit Pauline.

"What the hell are you doing here?"

His voice, squeezed through a constricted throat, sounded girlish and afraid, but he started toward the man, who turned and went stumbling pell-mell down the stairs. It was only a split second before Hal was after him, his fear vanished. This was his house, by God, and any nosy bartender who came prowling around was going to get the shit kicked out of him.

The bartender took the lower flight of stairs in two bounds and landed running, headed for the back door. Hal detoured past the fireplace and grabbed a bronze-headed poker from the rack, toppling the other tools as he did so. Armed with the poker, he ran into the kitchen, where the intruder was furiously trying to get the door unlocked.

"Hold it!" Hal commanded, raising his weapon. "One more move and I'll smash your head open with this."

The dark figure froze, hands on the doorknob, looking over his shoulder at Hal.

"Good. Now don't move."

Hal backed away, keeping his eyes on the man, groping with his left hand for the wall phone. Fear-filled eyes followed his movements. When his hand found the phone, Hal turned toward it.

That was a mistake. In the second it took him to glance away, the man sprang, both hands grasping the poker, wresting it free. But Hal had the phone. He brought it to his mouth and began jiggling the hook frantically. He was still jiggling it when the first blow struck.

He staggered into the painful brightness, lifting an arm and reaching desperately with his other hand for something, anything, wanting to inflict worse pain on the intruder. He banged into the table, a chair went over, he managed not to fall. The phone was his only hope. He tried to get to it, but the pain increased as he was struck again and again before descending into darkness.

SIXTEEN

Pauline preferred showers to baths except for one thing—she was always hearing noises with the water on, although when she turned it off there was only silence. Tonight was no different. She had turned the water off twice, and once even stepped dripping from the tub, held a towel in front of her, and cracked open the door into her bedroom to listen. Nothing but Linda Ronstadt.

After that, she resolved to ignore any noises she thought she heard. Lathering up, her head was suddenly full of a limerick Hal always recited when he barged in while she was bathing.

Miss Twye was soaping her breasts in the bath,
When she heard behind her a meaning laugh; To her
surprise she then discovered A wicked man in the
bathroom cupboard.

At which point Hal would lunge at her.

Pauline smiled—she couldn't help herself, not even now, when she could still feel the sting of Hal's hand on her face, still feel the dizzy sense of falling as she staggered across the lounge. It was crashing into those tables and then onto the floor that had bruised her thigh and skinned her elbow.

Andrew and Susannah had been right to get her out of the club, but once in the parking lot Pauline wished she had done something to injure Hal. It wasn't fair that he should strike her and not pay for it.

"You are the moral victor," Andrew assured her.

"File that divorce suit, Andrew. Immediately. I want to get it over with."

"I can't file it any earlier than tomorrow, which is when I intended to."

"Good!"

"I think Hal is going to fight it, Pauline. I thought you two had agreed this was the thing to do."

"When did Hal Stanfield ever keep his word about anything?"

Susannah took Pauline's elbow. "Come home with us, Pauline. Have a drink, calm down."

Pauline had always been half in love with Andrew Broom, and for that reason alone she would have disliked Susannah. But she disliked her on independent grounds as well. How could a woman who had been free and successful be so subservient to her husband, even if that husband was Andrew Broom?

"Thank you. I think I'll just go home."

"Good idea," Andrew said. "If you aren't already, tomorrow you and Hal will be officially adversaries. It might be a good thing to establish claim to the house."

"It was my father's house."

"I know that. But squatter's rights go a long way in property settlements."

Susannah touched her arm again, trying to be nice, and it was all Pauline could do not to pull her arm free. She felt that Susannah was patronizing her. Hal had put her in an impossibly vulnerable position. She looked back at the clubhouse, glowing white in the bright lights from the parking lot. Everyone in there must be laughing at her. Again, she felt an impulse to storm back in and have the final say in her argument with Hal, strike the final blow. He wouldn't *dare* hit her again.

Now, pleasantly punished by the pelting water, Pauline no longer felt as she had under the influence of that remembered limerick. She was the wronged woman, the innocent party. Official adversaries, Andrew had called them, and it had been fair warning. Trying to separate out what was hers from what was his was going to be a job for Solomon himself. Silvia was right. She should take Hal for all he was worth. What difference did it make that she was worth as much or more herself? Hal had traded on her family name, that had carried him in Wyler. Wasn't much of what he had made due to her anyway? It seemed self-evident to Pauline that it was.

She closed her eyes and lifted her face to the stinging water. Imaginary sounds assaulted her ears—movements on the stairs, a voice—but she shook her head, trying to ignore them, giving herself up to the sensation of water battering her face and breasts, running the length of her body. She would finish her shower and have as many drinks as it took to carry her into dreamless sleep.

The thought appealed to her, and she turned off the water, stepped from the tub, and put on her floor-length terry-cloth monk's robe, pulling the hood over her damp hair. Before she opened the door, she heard or thought she heard a voice, a shout, but there was only the sound of music from the speakers when she stepped into the bedroom. Imagination is a strange thing.

From downstairs came a crashing sound, as of something falling, and Pauline gasped in sudden fear. What had that been? The sound was too loud, too distinct, to dismiss as imaginary. She moved across the room as if on wires, her intention to shut and lock the bedroom door, but when she reached it, another sound came to her. The sound of a door closing.

Holding her breath, Pauline crept into the hall. She told herself it was Hal, and the thought brought relief before it brought anger. Had he slammed the door when he came in? Probably drunk as a lord. But what had been the other noise she heard?

She went down to the landing. Now she heard the sound of a key and then quite clearly the shooting of a bolt. It was the back door.

"Hal?" Her voice was timid, unreal. "Hal!"

No answer. It occurred to her that Hal had been in the house and left, and that meant he had come for something. What had he taken away? My God, the safe in the dining room!

Pauline ran down the stairs, her robe billowing open as she did, but she didn't care, she was suddenly certain that Hal had sneaked in while she was in the shower and cleaned out the safe. Some of her jewelry was there, what wasn't at the bank, and there were some stock certificates and— But what difference did it make?

She turned on the dining-room light, but there was no sign that the tapestry had been moved. Pulling her robe tightly about her, Pauline went around the table and lifted the tapestry away from the wall. The safe was closed. She let the tapestry drop. Fear started up again. Someone had been in the house. Perhaps someone still was. A prickly sensation ran over her scalp.

She should have used the telephone in her room before coming downstairs. The closest phone to her now was in the kitchen. She turned out the dining-room light and felt suddenly safer. Craning her neck, she looked into the kitchen. The receiver of the wall phone was off the hook. From it came a complaining sound, the warning that the line was open.

The sound was impossible to ignore. Pauline went into the kitchen to hang up the phone. She was reaching for it when she tripped over the body.

For a second time that night she was out of control and falling. She looked down, saw the body, and then her hand was in something sticky and warm and it was blood and she screamed, screamed as loud as she could, horrified, more frightened than she had ever been in her life, and when she scrambled to her feet and backed away, she saw the sickening mess that was the top of Hal's head and knew that he was dead. Instinctively, her hand went to her breast, her bloody hand, and her white terry-cloth robe wore splotches of red. She turned on the water in the sink to wash the blood off her hands, not knowing she was doing this. Lodged in her mind was the thought that she had to get to the phone.

She must phone for help. For the police. My God, her husband was dead. Murdered.

She stood at the sink with the cold water running on her extended hand and let that thought repeat itself in her mind. Hal was dead. Hal had been murdered. That she should feel a little leap of elation at that moment, thinking I am free, I am free, did not seem ghoulish, but her next thoughts were more cautious.

On the floor beside the body was a fireplace tool from the living room. Remembering the anger with which she had run downstairs, her fury at the thought that Hal was robbing her, she imagined herself picking up the poker before finding Hal rifling through the safe and striking him. For a crazy moment she was sure it had happened. Of course, it hadn't, but the thought would not go away. It stayed because it seemed to be what people would think. My God! After that scene at the club, this would look like her revenge. She began to wish she had gone home with Andrew and Susannah.

The surge of concern for herself, the realization that she could be thought responsible for what had happened to Hal, drained her mind of the fear that Hal's assailant might still be in the house. She turned off the water and, preoccupied, did not bother to dry her hands before crossing the room and replacing the receiver of the wall phone. She stared at the phone. She might telephone Andrew, ask if she could come speak with him, say she had been driving around since leaving the club...

The clock read eleven-fifteen. It was then that she thought of Silvia and relief flooded through her. It was not too late to go to Silvia, tell her of the fight at the club, say she did not want to go home for fear of meeting Hal.

She stepped over the body and ran toward the stairs, wanting to get out of the house as quickly as possible.

SEVENTEEN

ON THE BENCH Teufel settled back to listen to the opening statements, his manner suggesting that he considered this trial to be merely a formal concession to Duff Hogan's constitutional rights. The judge had ruled that Duff's confession was inadmissible and that the defendant's outburst during the preliminary hearing was never to be mentioned, despite the fact that the only paper any of the jurors read was the *Wyler Dealer,* which had been regularly referring to Duff Hogan as the self-confessed slayer of Larry Moss.

Yoder's opening statement made much of the fact that the jury must judge the defendant only on the basis of what was presented in the trial. As far as they were concerned, they had never known or heard of Duff Hogan until this moment. Think of him as a stranger. Yoder would present evidence that would convincingly prove that Duff Hogan was indeed the killer of Lawrence Moss. That "indeed" was masterful. But Andrew Broom did not lift so much as an eyebrow in protest.

Called upon to make his opening statement, Andrew rose and spoke to the jury from the defense table, Duff Hogan seated impassively next to him, Gerald on the far side of the defendant. Andrew said that he was in agreement with the prosecutor that Larry Moss was dead, but that was about the extent of their agreement. The prosecutor would be unable to produce a murder weapon. The prosecution's case was built on hearsay, and it would be the task of the defense to establish the untrustworthiness of the statement on which that case was built. Then Duff Hogan would appear as what he was, innocent of any crime whatsoever, let alone the murder of Larry Moss.

Before getting started, Yoder wanted a conference and they approached the bench.

"Is Hogan's statement now admissible, Your Honor?"

"You know my ruling on that," Teufel said querulously.

"But Broom made all but explicit reference to it in his opening statement, Your Honor." Spittle had a way of forming in the corners of Yoder's wide mouth, lending a mad note to whatever he said.

"I made no open reference," Andrew said.

"Everyone in the courtroom knows what you meant."

"Indeed?"

Teufel's frown deepened. "That's enough. My ruling stands. Let's get going."

Yoder began by establishing that Larry Moss was in fact dead. The coroner made it official. It was only when, with Cleary on the stand, the prosecutor attempted to show that Moss had been murdered that Andrew began to object.

Were there any witnesses to the crime? Yoder treated the question with contempt but did not enjoy having his reaction explicitly interpreted as an admission that no one had seen Moss killed.

"Well, he was certainly dead," Yoder snorted, rolling his eyes at the jury.

"That you have successfully established," Broom agreed.

Yoder asked Cleary a series of questions meant to establish that there was no possible doubt Larry Moss had been murdered, but the sheriff seemed determined not to make Yoder's job any easier. Like Teufel, Cleary appeared to have no doubt of the outcome of the trial and thus could afford to sin on the side of fairness to the defendant. Before Yoder was through with him, Cleary testified that everything at the scene where the body was found was consistent with death having been brought about by foul play.

"Your witness," Yoder said, apparently satisfied.

"I couldn't agree more," Andrew Broom said, advancing toward Cleary as to an ally. "Tell me, Sheriff, what led you to the spot where the body was found?"

Yoder objected, Teufel sustained him. There was another huddle before the bench with the prosecutor maintaining that if the defense kept referring to Hogan's confession the prosecution should be able to use it too. Broom said nothing. Teufel repeated his ruling, looking meaningfully at Andrew. "I know defense counsel would do nothing that would jeopardize his client."

Andrew assured him the assumption was correct. He resumed questioning the witness.

"Sheriff Cleary, did some informant tell you that a body could be found where the body of Larry Moss was found?"

"Yes."

"And otherwise you would not have found the body?"

"I might not have, but it would have been found. I've already described how we found it, just covered with leaves, not buried."

"As if it was meant to be discovered?"

Cleary shrugged. "I don't know about that."

"But you discovered it."

"Well, Duff took us out there—"

Teufel's gavel hit his desk, Yoder sprang to his feet, but Andrew beat him to the bench. "Your Honor, I'm afraid you must either declare a mistrial or change your ruling on introducing my client's confession.''

Teufel asked that the jury be taken from the courtroom and, when they were gone, glowered at Andrew.

"I am not going to call a mistrial, Counselor. What I am going to do is instruct the witness to make no further allusions to Duff Hogan's confession.''

"The fat is in the fire, Your Honor,'' Yoder said.

"Are *you* asking for a mistrial?''

"He's right, Your Honor,'' Andrew said. "We cannot erase the remark from the jury's minds. Either a mistrial or the confession will have to be discussed.''

"You *want* it discussed,'' Yoder said, genuinely puzzled.

"What I want is neither here nor there. What's it to be, Your Honor?''

"If I change my ruling, you will immediately file for a mistrial, won't you?''

Andrew Broom looked expressionlessly at the judge. "No, Your Honor.''

"Very well. Bailiff, bring back the jury.''

When the jury was settled, the judge told Andrew to proceed.

"Sheriff, you were telling us that Duff Hogan led you to the body.''

"That's right.''

"Did he explain why you would find a body at that spot?''

"He said he'd buried it there.''

"And you believed him?''

Cleary smiled. "An examination of the defendant's shoes indicated that he had been in the area before. His fingernails concealed dirt that matched dirt at the spot where the body was found.''

"Would you say that constitutes sufficient proof that the defendant buried the body?"

"Yes."

"Why did he do that?"

"Why did he bury it?"

"Yes."

"To conceal it."

"You mean until he had come to lead you out to where the body was concealed?"

"I guess so."

"How much time elapsed between the burial and the defendant's coming to you to say he knew where you would find a body?"

"Death had occurred approximately twenty-four hours earlier."

"I didn't ask you that, Sheriff. I asked how much time elapsed between the burial and the discovery."

Cleary shook his head. "Twenty-four hours?"

"Only if we assume that the body was buried by Duff Hogan immediately after death. Why should we assume that?"

"He said he killed the boy."

"Ah."

"He said he killed him and would show us where the body was buried."

"You believed him?"

"Everything fit."

"You mean you have proof? Proof like the dirt under the fingernails and the mud on the shoes?"

"He said he did it."

"Yes, I know. He said he buried the body and you were able to establish that independently of what he told you. Were you able to establish independently of his confession that Duff Hogan killed Larry Moss?"

Of course, Cleary did not want to answer no, but neither could he cite evidence that Duff had killed Larry Moss. The coroner had testified that the body had died of strangulation. Strangled with a rope.

"I don't believe the rope was placed in evidence, Sheriff."

"No, sir."

"Was the rope ever found?"

"No, sir."

"Did you ask Duff Hogan if he knew where the rope was?"

"He said he threw it away."

"I see. Where did he claim to have thrown the rope?"

"In the river."

"In the river. Why would he do that?"

"So it wouldn't be found."

"Yet he came to tell you where the body was. What exactly are we to think, Sheriff? Was Duff Hogan trying to conceal this death or planning to come to you and claim to have caused it?"

Yoder objected, suggesting that the defense could put Hogan on the stand and satisfy his curiosity about these matters.

"Your Honor, I am trying to understand the case the prosecutor has brought. I am trying to discover whether any evidence was found suggesting that Duff Hogan caused the death of Larry Moss. I gather the answer is no."

"He said he did it," Sheriff Cleary said.

"Yes, he did. And I am now glad that has been mentioned. Let me review your testimony, Sheriff. Duff Hogan told you he had buried the dead body of Larry Moss, right?"

"Yes."

"You didn't simply take his word for that. You examined his nails, you sent his shoes to Indianapolis, and established that he had indeed been at that spot before and that he had dug in the earth."

"Yes."

"He also told you he had killed Larry Moss?"

"Yes."

"But you were unable to find evidence of the truth of this claim, is that right?"

Yoder objected, but Teufel instructed Cleary to answer the question and the answer was no.

"Thank you. Now then, what motive did Duff Hogan tell you he had to kill Larry Moss?"

"He said that he sexually assaulted him."

"He said that?"

"Yes."

"He volunteered that?"

"He admitted it. He included it in his statement."

"But was he the first to bring it up?"

"I'm not sure."

"Nonetheless, as you say, he mentioned that motive in his confession. Answer this question, Sheriff. Did you do anything to prove or disprove that portion of the confession?"

"His clothing was sent to Indianapolis."

"Was there any evidence of sexual assault?"

Cleary shifted in the witness chair. "Not on the body, no. But it is possible—"

"No guesses, Sheriff. Any signs on Duff Hogan that anything like that had happened?"

"Not on the clothes he was wearing."

"Are you suggesting he might have changed?"

"I don't know."

"Surely, that must have occurred to you."

"It did."

"Did you test other clothing of the defendant's?"

All Duff's clothing found at the Hogan home had been sent to Indianapolis with similar negative results. Mrs. Hogan would testify that none of her son's clothing was missing. The coroner had made no mention of sexual assault when he described the body. Did Sheriff Cleary think it worthwhile to recall the coroner to see if he had perhaps overlooked something in his report? Cleary said the coroner had left nothing out.

"Sheriff, what do you think of the prosecutor's bringing Duff Hogan to trial with no evidence of guilt?"

"Objection, Your Honor!"

"Withdraw the question. Thank you, Sheriff Cleary. I have no further questions for this witness."

EIGHTEEN

GERALD FOLLOWED his uncle's courtroom performance with fascination. Andrew had maneuvered to get the confession mentioned and then used it to undermine the prosecution's case. To weaken it, anyway. But it was difficult to see what effect he was having on the jury. Twelve expressionless midwestern faces followed the questioning with interest but gave no clue as to how they thought the trial was going.

Yoder would keep insisting on the fact that Duff had buried the body, putting him at the scene of the crime, and, more important, the fact that he had confessed to killing the boy. Still, the jury would have to wonder why the sheriff had been unable to prove the crucial part of the case against Duff.

A case that looked doomed suddenly had taken on at least an even chance of acquittal. Andrew had never approached the case as mere routine, cut and dried, a matter of seeing that Duff got a fair trial. Nor had he volunteered just for the exercise, to see if he could get a jury to throw out a case against someone manifestly guilty. Andrew Broom believed Duff Hogan was innocent.

Why? Because of Duff's religion, Andrew had said.

"Don't you think Catholics ever murder?"

"I think this Catholic didn't."

"Because there is no direct evidence?"

"There is no direct evidence that he committed sexual assault because he did not do it. *Modus tollens.*"

Gerald could not decide whether his uncle was serious or not. Of course, it made logical sense to say that if something had not been done, there could not be any evidence it had been done, but in the law the procedure was the reverse. If there is no evidence, the assumption has to be that the deed was not done.

"Why did he confess?"

Andrew smiled. "Because he's a Catholic."

Seated next to Gerald, Duff Hogan followed the proceedings closely enough but betrayed no emotion as he did so. Was the pudgy defendant innocent or guilty? Gerald found it impossible not to be affected by the fact that Duff had confessed to the crime. Nor could he look at that porcine profile and see a moral hero, sacrificing himself for . . . for what? That was the flaw in Uncle Andrew's theory.

Thank God Andrew did not have to prove his theory. His task as defense attorney only required him to refute the theory of the prosecution.

A folded piece of paper was put on the table in front of Gerald. After he unfolded and read it, he turned to see Susannah standing just inside the padded courtroom doors. She beckoned to him, a desperate expression on her face. Gerald got up and went swiftly in a half crouch toward the door. Susannah had opened it, and he continued right on into the hall, feeling a bit like Groucho Marx.

"How's it going, Gerald?"

"Okay."

She held his eyes with her intense expression. "Something awful has happened. Something terrible. Hal Stanfield is dead. It looks as if he was murdered."

Gerald stared at her. Sheriff Cleary was still in the courtroom.

"How do you know that?"

"Pauline called and told me. She wants Andrew to come see her immediately."

"He's a little busy right now."

"I explained that to her and she became hysterical."

"I gather she hasn't notified the police."

"She wants to talk to Andrew first."

"Is she home?"

"She says she won't talk to anyone but Andrew."

"Well, that's just too damned bad. If she has knowledge a crime has been committed, she had better report it as soon as possible. I'm going over there."

He could see he was doing exactly what Susannah hoped he would do. He tried to derive some satisfaction from that on his way to the Stanfield house, but he had little reason to think he would be able to get Pauline Stanfield to do anything she didn't want to do.

She was waiting in a car beside the house and glared at him when, having parked behind her, he came up to the window on the driver's side.

"Where's the body?"

"Inside. Where is Andrew Broom?"

"In court. Is the door unlocked?"

"Why lock it?"

The door was slightly ajar and, pushing it open, Gerald felt a wave of apprehension. He did not have to go far before he saw what he would have preferred not to see. Hal Stanfield lay in a heap beneath the wall phone in the kitchen. Gerald tried not to look at the soupy mess of the head as he made the call. Landers answered.

"This is Gerald Rowan. I'm calling from the Stanfield residence. There's a dead body here, looks like murder."

"Quit kidding, Rowan."

"I'm serious. Cleary was still in the courtroom when I left."

"You going to be there when we get there?"

Gerald hung up and went outside. Mrs. Stanfield had driven back to the garage, turned around and was now coming down the drive. Gerald put up his hand, but she swerved out over the lawn in order to go around his car. He caught up to her as she was coming back onto the driveway before going into the street. He pulled open the passenger door, and she took her foot off the gas as he slipped in beside her.

"Where we going?"

"I want to talk to Andrew Broom."

"Look, he's in court. There's no way he can talk to you now. We better stay here until the sheriff comes."

"I don't want to say anything until I talk to Andrew."

"Did you do it?"

Her eyes narrowed with contempt. "I suppose I should have expected that. I spent the night with a friend. I came home a half hour ago and found what you found. I have been waiting here for Andrew Broom, but you came instead."

"You call from the kitchen?"

"What do you mean?"

"Did you phone the office from the kitchen?"

She looked at him in exaggerated disbelief. "Is that all you want to know? You find a dead body and all you want to know is where I phoned from?"

The sheriff's car came wheeling around the corner, followed by an ambulance. Cleary saw them in the car, and came puffing up to the driver's window. He touched the brim of his hat.

"Where?"

"In the kitchen."

The medical examiner came, then more deputies, and before Healy of the *Dealer* showed up, Gerald had heard Pauline Stanfield's story. As Gerald must know—the whole town must know—there had been a terrible fight at the club last night; Hal had struck her in public, humiliating her. She had left, refusing the offer to go home with Andrew and Susannah, but when she got home she thought better of it and called Silvia and asked if she could spend the night with her. She did, and when she came home, she found the body of her husband.

Meaning she must have telephoned the office on the kitchen phone with the body of her husband on the floor at her feet. For some reason that seemed significant to Gerald Rowan.

NINETEEN

BARANY WAS barreling down the Wabash Road half a mile from home before he really thought of what the hell he was doing. The sight of his house, lit up like a Christmas tree, snapped him out of it, because for a moment he didn't remember turning on those lights. It gave him something to do when he had the car in the garage and got inside the house, turning off all the lights. In the dark, he stripped off the jogging suit and that made his shivering seem okay, but after a while he put on a robe and sat in the middle of the couch in the living room, hugged himself with both arms, and stared out the window toward the Wabash Road.

I killed the wrong Stanfield, he thought, and then he said it aloud. "I killed the wrong Stanfield."

He began to laugh, forcing it at first, then laughing effortlessly; it really was funny when you stopped to think of it. After all those weeks of brooding and planning to take care of *her,* everything fell apart and he ended up killing *him.*

He reviewed every moment from the time Noreen had dropped him off, the driving into Wyler, parking, letting himself into the Stanfield house, going upstairs to the sound of muted music, and waiting in the den for the right moment.

After the fight at the club he hadn't expected to see Stanfield. Could he have avoided running into him in the hallway? In retrospect, he could think of a dozen ways he could have gotten out of the house undetected and put off his plan to another day. But he had decided to go for the stairs as soon as he knew Stanfield was on the second floor. And just as he got to them, Stanfield emerged from the bedroom and they were staring at one another. God, what a shock. Leo went down those stairs as fast as he could, but when he hit the back door and found it locked, he had been almost out of his mind trying to get it open, and then Stanfield came at him with that poker.

Barany's arm lifted now as it had after he wrested the poker from Stanfield's hand, and he brought it down again and again as he had in the kitchen, feeling the sickening give of Stanfield's skull but not wanting to stop until he had killed him. Stanfield had recognized him in the upstairs hallway, no doubt about it, and once the man came after him, Barany had no choice. He had to kill him.

Now, sitting on the sofa in his darkened living room, hugging himself, staring out at the dusty driveway barely visible as it trailed down to the Wabash Road, he tried to figure out what might happen next.

Thinking of the Stanfield house, he closed his eyes and retraced his steps through the rooms, up the stairs and down, reviewed the struggle with Stanfield, trying to think if he had left any clue to the fact that he had been there, that he was the one who had killed Stanfield. He told himself there was nothing, no way in the world anyone could connect him with the house or the killing.

He had no known motive. That was to have been the beauty of killing *her*. No one would know the reason he had for doing that. She didn't know, nobody knew. He had been very careful that no link be established between them. Taking the job at the country club had been risky, but there was no more reason to connect him to the

Stanfields than anyone else who worked in the club—say, Noreen.

No, he had no fear that suspicion would fall on him. But he took no comfort from the thought. His caution had been aimed at getting rid of that contemptible woman. Now he had wasted it all by killing her husband and, if the fight were any indication, actually doing her a favor in the process.

He could not sleep. He listened to the radio throughout the night, to demented disk jockeys, to talk shows of unbelievable earthiness, to the constant din of a music whose target seemed the whole body rather than the ear. There were newsbreaks constantly but nothing about Stanfield. No mention at all of a body being found or a break-in reported.

Toward dawn he fell asleep on the sofa and came awake at nine when a weak ray of sun played over his stubbled face. He had fallen over onto his side, and when he straightened, he realized his back had been twisted as he slept. He felt a sudden pain as he sat up, straining his back.

The memory of what he had done to Stanfield with that poker came rushing at him and he tried to dismiss it as a bad dream. Killing was only tolerable when the memory of it became dreamlike. But this killing wasn't like the others. He tugged his robe around him, rose, and was unable to stand erect because of the pain in his back. He moved like an old man into the kitchen, where he poured himself a glass of Cranapple juice and turned on the radio.

But it was now six minutes past the hour and he had missed the news. He twisted the dial angrily but without any luck. It was not until ten o'clock that he got the local news on a Wyler station.

Nothing.

Absolutely nothing. What the hell was going on? He imagined Mrs. Stanfield still upstairs, unaware that the dead body of her husband lay on the kitchen floor. Was it possible that the body had not been discovered?

He telephoned the Stanfield house, telling himself this was stupid, but he didn't intend to say anything, only find out if she would answer. No one answered. He let the phone ring on and on before finally putting it down. What was she up to?

For months his mind had been full of her, but never before had she seemed menacing. He did not know how the balance had shifted, only that he had put power into her hands. He felt that she was toying with him now.

He dressed and went out to his car and drove toward Wyler. If the phone call was stupid, this was insane, but he had to see what was going on, find out why the death had not been reported. On the way to Wyler, he listened to the radio, cursing the stupid chatter and inane music. Why didn't they tell their listeners what was going on in their goddam town? The eleven o'clock news came on just as he arrived in Wyler, but the lead story dealt with the trial of Duff Hogan for the murder of Larry Moss. Was it possible Stanfield's death would play second fiddle to that? No. Stanfield's murder wasn't mentioned at all.

As Barany approached the house, a car came down the street from the direction of downtown and pulled into the Stanfield driveway. Driving slowly by, Barany saw the other car in the driveway. He continued on to town and was having a cup of coffee in Osco's Drugs when someone ran out of the sheriff's office and jumped into a car. Two minutes later the ambulance went by. Barany signaled the waitress and asked for an order of raisin toast.

TWENTY

ANDREW BROOM got a first and hurried account of what had happened to Hal Stanfield from Gerald during the luncheon break. It was depressing how easy it was to think of Hal as dead.

"Pauline demands to talk with you, Andrew."

At the moment, Susannah was with her in the law library of the suite of offices on the twelfth floor of the Hoosier Towers. Duff Hogan was being fed by the sheriff. Andrew did not want any distraction from Duff's trial.

"How's she taking it?"

"She's not hysterical."

"What do you think happened, Gerald?"

"To Hal? I don't know. A break-in, I suppose, and he unwisely confronted the guy."

"How was he dressed?"

"Up. A suit, necktie. Maybe the guy was in the house when he came home."

"Have they established a time of death?"

"Over twelve hours, going by body temperature."

"Twelve hours from when?"

"From about eleven."

Pauline had left the club with Susannah and himself at nine the night before. He said to Gerald, "Find out exactly when Hal left the country club last night."

Gerald nodded, but he looked as if he wanted to ask why. It was a good thing he didn't. Andrew would not have known what to answer.

"Cleary will check with Silvia."

"Check what?"

"That Pauline was there. Did you hear about their fight?"

Andrew told him what had happened, possibly as a corrective to Pauline's version. As he did so, he imagined Yoder fashioning a case against Pauline. Not only was Hal threatening to thwart her desire for a divorce, he had struck her in public, humiliating her. The Stanfield marriage alone provided her with years of motivation for killing Hal. Andrew could easily imagine Pauline taking a poker to her husband. It was a good thing she had not been in the house when Hal was killed.

"What happened in court after I left?" Gerald asked.

"When did you leave?"

"You were making the point that no evidence had been found to corroborate Duff's claim to have killed Larry Moss."

"I hope the jury got the point."

"But now it will be part of the trial record that Duff did confess. They'll ask why he said he did if he didn't."

Andrew nodded. "Why do people confess to crimes they didn't commit?"

"Crazy?"

"Sometimes. More often because they're protecting someone."

"You think Duff knows who killed Larry Moss?"

Andrew looked at Gerald. Just like that, he had it. Of course. It fit perfectly. He pushed back from his desk and stood.

"What time is it?" he asked his watch as he pushed back his cuff. It was twelve-fifty. The trial would resume at two.

"Is your car downstairs?"

"Why?"

"Come on."

He didn't want to voice it, not yet, but he was certain he had hit upon the key. Of course Duff was protecting someone, protecting them from what as a Catholic he would regard as the worst sin of all. They went down in the elevator but not alone, and that helped because Gerald couldn't press him with Clem the maintenance man in the elevator with them. Clem was the nosiest man on God's green earth. Once he had brought some papers to Andrew's office saying he was sure he hadn't meant to throw them away. It was the draft of a will. It had been thrown out. It seemed clear Clem inspected the building's trash before letting it be carried away. Andrew invested in a shredder. It went without saying that nothing could be said in Clem's presence.

But once they were in the car, Andrew said, "Go out Tarkington to Twelfth, then take a right."

"Where we going?"

"To the river."

"The river?"

"The scene of the crime."

Let Gerald think this was a routine visit, a little refreshener before returning to court.

Out of the office, away from downtown, on a beautiful summer day, Andrew would have given anything to be on his way to Walnut Grove and an afternoon of golf. While Duff Hogan's fate was being decided in a courtroom downtown, people were hitting approach shots, going to the beach, or, as was clear when Gerald brought his car across the bumpy terrain to where the body of Larry Moss had been found, fishing in the Wabash River.

An old man in a flat-bottomed boat sat with his pole parallel to the water, the picture of summertime indolence. Andrew got out of the car and walked toward the river as if he wanted a better look at the fisherman in the boat. But he walked directly to the spot where the dead body of Larry Moss had been uncovered. Dead. Strangled with a rope. Andrew looked down at the ground and then lifted his head and looked straight up.

The tree was a pine, a fairly large one, its lower branches sizable, maybe four to six inches in diameter. A good climbing tree. The branches seemed to form a spiral staircase that led up into a needled sky. Andrew was interested in the branch just above him.

"Give me a hand, Gerald."

"You want to climb the tree?"

"That's right."

"Why?"

"I hope to tell you in a minute."

Gerald made a kind of stirrup with his hands, Andrew eased his loafer into it, then Gerald gave a heave and Andrew was lifted to a point where he could grab the branch. He swung his foot to a lower branch jutting from the trunk at right angles to the branch he held, and soon he was looking down at the branch that was directly over the spot where the body was found. He leaned forward to get a closer look. He smiled grimly. There was little doubt of it. The bark bore unmistakable marks of a rope. In a minute, Andrew was on the ground next to Gerald.

"Well?" Gerald asked.

"Now I know who Duff is protecting."

"Who?"

"Larry Moss."

TWENTY-ONE

GERALD ROWAN was cute and not all that much younger than she was, but Silvia had made up her mind not to mix business with monkey business when it came to dealing with her lawyer. At first, she had thought of him as only second best—Hal had assured her he would arrange for Andrew Broom to handle her affairs and getting the nephew had been a disappointment—but Silvia had learned that the boyish lawyer knew it all. In a bookish way, that is—he hadn't had much experience. But all in all, she was content with Gerald.

Talking with Gerald the day after Hal Stanfield was killed was different. She had slept until noon and then lazed around the apartment after telephoning her various parlors.

"Has Cleary talked with you yet?"

"The sheriff? Why would he want to talk with me?"

"Mrs. Stanfield says she spent the night at your place."

"Is that a crime?"

"She had a fight with her husband."

"I know."

It had been quite a surprise when Pauline showed up not an hour after her husband had left. Apparently, she had not gone home from the country club after all.

"I've been driving around ever since leaving the club," Pauline had said, taking the bourbon on the rocks as if it alone stood between her and a nervous breakdown. "The Brooms wanted me to go home with them, but I wanted to be alone. Now I don't. Silvia, can I stay here tonight?"

She could hardly throw her out. Of course she could stay. That meant Silvia had to endure hours of Pauline's version of what happened at the club. Hal had belted her, that was clear. Listening to Pauline's repeated description of that blow was about the only fun Silvia got out of the tale.

"When did she get here?" Gerald Rowan asked.

It wasn't until then, believe it or not, that Silvia realized these were strange questions.

"Why do you ask?"

"Mr. Stanfield was killed last night."

"Come on."

"At his home. What time did Pauline get here?"

"When was he killed?"

Gerald smiled. "Answer my question and I'll answer yours."

That is what it seemed to be, a game they were playing. It wasn't possible that Hal was dead. He had been here last night, they had talked, they had gone to bed together and smoked pot, he had gone home to make sure the fight did not bring on a divorce. It was also as an aspect of the game that Silvia first saw the significance of Gerald's question. Had Pauline spent the night with her only to establish an alibi?

"It was late. Midnight? Pauline will remember."

"It would help if you could."

"I'd say midnight." Silvia was pretty sure it had been later, closer to twelve-thirty. "When was Hal killed?"

Later it seemed unbelievable to her that she had been able to go on chatting like that. Gerald had actually seen the body and he told her about it, but of course he had no way of knowing that he was talking about someone she had slept with last night, just hours before he died. She listened as if it were some story Gerald was making up. They could only guess when Hal had died.

"You think Pauline killed him?"

"Not if she was with you."

"She was here, but even if she weren't, she couldn't have done a thing like that."

"Anyone can do anything. I quote my Uncle Andrew."

Silvia could not imagine Pauline hitting Hal with a poker, not hard enough to kill him, and anyhow, he wouldn't have let her do it.

"Where is Pauline now?"

"Cleary is talking with her. It's just routine."

What else could it be? Still, Silvia was a little disappointed as the realization sank in that her daydreams about snaring Hal after Pauline divorced him would never come true. It was as if Pauline had cheated her of that possibility.

"Who would have killed Hal Stanfield?"

Gerald looked at her. "If you had known him very well, you wouldn't ask."

"What do you mean?"

"He was not an easy man to like. I don't think he was short on enemies."

She asked him to tell her again how Hal's body had looked, crumpled on the kitchen floor. What would Gerald Rowan say if he knew that Hal had been there last night and then gone home to get killed? If only she had made him stay with her! Oh sure, and then have Pauline show up and want to spend the night. What a trio they would have made. Someone would have been killed for sure then, probably Silvia.

Was there any way anyone could know Hal had been with her last night? The fact that Pauline had spent the night should have been more reassuring than it was, but Silvia had no illusions that she would be treated the way Pauline Stanfield was. The owner of some tanning parlors, new to town, what would it sound like if it became known that she and Hal had been lovers? Silvia didn't want to find out, that was for sure. Who could connect her with Hal?

Other tenants must have seen him enter the building, but then he owned the place and they might not have wondered about it. Silvia had kept quiet about Hal and herself. In large part, that was just her way. She didn't believe in letting others in on her personal life, if only because she didn't want to give them ammunition against her. She had never talked to anyone about Hal Stanfield. But the thought drifted away as she tried to hang on to it.

Noreen. The blonde who waited tables at the country club. She had talked with the girl about Pauline, that was certain, but had they talked of Hal too?

But the more she thought of it, business rather than pleasure would link her with Hal Stanfield. He might be able to cover his tracks as a lover, but he was sure to have kept records of the money he had put into her parlors.

TWENTY-TWO

CLEARY BROUGHT DUFF from his cell and left him with Andrew. The lawyer told his client what he had learned.

"That's what happened, isn't it, Duff? You found that boy hanging there like Judas Iscariot and you cut him down and covered the body with leaves and told a fantastic story just to keep it from his family."

Fat body, fat face, even his eyes looked fat as he followed what Andrew Broom said. However unrevealing the rotund rest of him might be, the eyes had it. Andrew could see he had hit upon the explanation. The question now was whether Duff was a fat-head too and would attempt to stick to his story.

"Duff, it's unfortunate and tragic and all the rest, but God hasn't put you or me in charge of the universe. And let's give the Mosses some credit. If you can live with the knowledge of what happened, don't you think they can too?"

It took twenty minutes, and Duff was a lot harder than most juries. Maybe the key was arguing that there are two kinds of suicide, intended and unintended.

"Unintended suicide may seem a contradiction in terms, Duff, but I can show you experts who feel most suicides are in a way accidents. Ever try to imagine yourself dead? It's almost impossible to do. The best most of us can do is imagine ourselves living in different circumstances. That is what most so-called suicides want, a change of venue."

Bad. Never use legal jargon with a civilian.

If it had not been for the way Duff's eyes were fixed on him, Andrew could not have kept it up, talking without any verbal reply.

"Duff, you and I believe that people go on after death. Most people do believe that. But in ways which make a mockery out of life. You're a bastard all your life and then die and step into light and bliss. Duff, you and I will go from that county courtroom to another, to a judge who can't be fooled and won't even let us fool ourselves, not then, not anymore. When you saw Larry hanging there, you thought of heaven and hell and his immortal soul, didn't you?"

Duff began to nod and now his eyes were moist.

"Of course you did. But you aren't God, Duff. Neither am I. Let's not judge that boy. He probably thought he was just pretending, trying it out, and then he slipped and it was over, but he didn't mean it."

"What if he did?"

"We're not God."

Those twenty minutes were not wasted; they served as a rehearsal for Duff's testimony when Andrew put him on the stand that afternoon. Yoder accepted this reversal calmly enough, probably because he was already preoccupied with the death of Hal Stanfield. Not that he just rolled over. Cleary had been back to the place by the river and verified that a rope had been tied to the branch above the spot where the body was found.

"How do we know Duff Hogan didn't hang the boy and then bury him. Why should we believe him?"

"For the same reason you brought him to trial in the first place. He says so. Then you tried to believe a fantastic confession, but you know you believe what he says now."

He had to withdraw it, of course, but he got it into his final statement. Yoder might have wanted a mistrial, but old Teufel lived in dread of a reversal by a higher court and they played it out to the end.

The case against Duff Hogan was dismissed.

Duff was more relieved by the fact that afterward Mr. Moss shook his hand and Mrs. Moss took him in her arms as if he were the son she had lost. Tears poured out of Duff's tiny eyes and ran down his fat face. It occurred to Andrew that, by his own lights, Duff had done as much for another as he could. It was an odd thought, but one he did not care to dismiss, that Duff Hogan was in his own way a moral hero.

Andrew himself could have enjoyed the outcome more if he did not have the death of Hal Stanfield to worry about. Yoder wanted to talk about what had happened to Hal right away, probably to ease the pain of losing the case, but Andrew was wary. Unless Gerald had found out something that pointed in another direction, he and Yoder might meet again in the same courtroom, deciding the fate of Pauline Stanfield.

He turned away from Yoder to Susannah, who stood by the defendant's table. Their eyes met and Andrew once more felt wonder that this woman, who had worked for him for years, had been an attractive efficient office appliance, had metamorphosed so completely into the most important person in his life. He went to her and took her hand and they headed back to the office. He would have liked to be heading somewhere altogether different with her, some vacation resort, an Aegean island. By God, he would even settle for the much advertised weekend at the Holiday Inn in Elkhart, Indiana.

Maybe the Hal Stanfield death was not as bad as it seemed.

But it was worse, far worse, than he had permitted himself to think. This made Pauline's reaction all the harder to take. She seemed to think that now that he was free of the Duff Hogan defense, he could just snap his fingers and get her out of this.

"Andrew, I have the definite feeling that they think I did this."

"You didn't, did you?"

"Andrew!"

"I want to hear it, Pauline, no matter how ridiculous it seems to you."

"Of course I didn't!"

"Fine. Now you're angry and that's good. Together we have to make very sure that no one else can think otherwise. Whether or not they suspect you now, unless something has turned up I don't know about, they will try to build a case against you. Whether they can get an indictment, let alone put together a coherent case, I don't know. But we are going to do everything we can to make sure that the first does not happen and, if it does, that the second does not."

THEY WERE in Andrew's office—Pauline, Susannah, Gerald, and Andrew—seated comfortably in what Andrew called his parlor—easy chairs and a sofa arranged around a table whose top was a great marble disc. It was less than half an hour since Duff's case had been dismissed.

"Oh, if only I had gone home with the two of you last night," Pauline said.

Andrew did not like it that she was in so much need of an alibi, but it was well to start with the worst view of her predicament.

"Pauline, I know you've already talked to others, to Gerald, to the sheriff..."

Pauline inhaled through her nostrils. "I would not answer a single one of that man's insinuating questions."

"Gerald's?"

It took a moment for her to see he was kidding. She put her hand on Gerald's sleeve. "Gerald was a dear. I meant that awful sheriff."

"It's his job."

"The nerve of that nobody, asking me to account for every minute, every second."

"I'm glad you didn't talk to him, Pauline. But we are going to talk now. Let me put it into context. Think of it as a game if that helps. The game is this. We're going to imagine Yoder the prosecutor thinking you killed Hal. His thinking it doesn't mean anything, of course, not by itself, so he will look for things, events, whatever, things done and said, that will lead people to believe you killed Hal. By people I mean a dozen locals who will sit in a jury box over in the courthouse. Our job is to find ways of responding to what Yoder tells that jury so they will continue to see you as innocent."

Maybe it is manipulative, but the best way to get people through things is to cast them in a role. It's what preachers do at a wedding. You are the bride, you are the groom. Somehow people know what is expected of them when you tell them the part they are playing. I am a mourner at the funeral of my father. It seems something anyone might do, only this time it is I and I must do it well. So it was that Pauline Stanfield took up the role of chief suspect in her husband's murder.

Not fifteen minutes went by before Andrew came to believe that it was a role Pauline would play in court.

First, the divorce. After years of threatening one another with divorce, Pauline had actually initiated action. Whereupon Hal decided he would fight it tooth and nail.

"But, Andrew, that isn't public knowledge."

"Anything and everything is public knowledge now, Pauline. Besides, your suit for divorce was filed this morning."

"This morning!"

"That's right."

"When Hal was already dead?" Pauline wore an awed look.

"We'll get back to that."

Second was the fight at the club. No question about that being public knowledge. Hal had knocked her across the lounge after a noisy argument. What spouse would not want revenge after such humiliation? Again Pauline said she wished she had accepted the Brooms' offer to spend the night with them.

"We left the club at nine-thirty. Does that establish when you left?"

She stared at him. "But I left at the same time as you and Susannah. We left together."

"And parted in the parking lot. You drove directly home?"

"I didn't drive home at all. My mind was in a whirl. I wanted to think and couldn't. Nothing like that had ever happened before. Hal had an awful temper, but he had never hit me. And then to do it in front of all those people!"

"Guess how long you drove around."

"Until I went to Silvia's."

Andrew turned to Gerald. "When did Pauline arrive at Silvia's?"

"She's not absolutely sure. Twelve or twelve-thirty."

Pauline did not seem to see the significance of this, meaning she was either dumb or shrewd. She certainly wasn't dumb, and she could have taught used car salesmen about shrewdness.

"That leaves you out driving around somewhere while Hal was killed. The prosecutor is going to suggest you went home, killed Hal, and then went to Silvia's."

"But I didn't! It's not true."

"And our job is to make sure people see that you didn't kill him. We're going to have to do better than saying you were driving around for two hours trying to think. So let's start there. You're going to have to remember that drive."

Now she was really angry at him. Andrew didn't blame her, but at least she now realized what a spot she was in. Not that she didn't fight it.

"Andrew, I haven't been arrested. Nobody has accused me of anything. Does a person have to prove she's innocent?"

"Let's call it a day then. But I want you to try to reconstruct the time between leaving the club and getting to Silvia's. You weren't drunk, were you?"

"I've never been drunk in my life."

"Do me a favor, Pauline. Don't say that under oath."

"What's that supposed to mean?"

Susannah said, "Where will she stay, Andrew?"

"I can't stay in that house."

Well, Andrew sure as hell did not want her staying with them. He conveyed this to Susannah with a glance.

"How about with Silvia?"

"No."

When Pauline went to powder her nose, Andrew made it explicit that he did not want his client for a house-guest.

"What do you think of her story, Susannah?"

"She's lying."

"I know."

"About what?" Gerald asked.

"The two-hour drive, for one thing. Susannah, you and Gerald get Pauline settled in a hotel. I want to talk with some of the people at the club."

Pauline came back looking as people do who know they have been discussed in their absence.

Andrew said, "Pauline, I want you incommunicado. The best way to ensure that is to put you in a hotel. Gerald will book a room at the Ben Hur in the name of one of my Chicago clients. He'll give you the key and you just go up there."

"I'll feel like a call girl."

Susannah took Pauline's arm. "What should I bring you from home, Pauline?"

Andrew and Gerald adjourned to the library.

"Anything else I should know, Gerald? I wish we'd had a chance to talk before that session."

"You laid it out for her."

"Yeah."

"A sort of sad note. Apparently, Hal had mixed a nightcap he didn't get a chance to drink. It was in the bedroom."

"Upstairs."

"The master bedroom."

"A last scotch?"

"It was bourbon."

There were only two things wrong with that, Andrew thought as he drove to the club. Hal never drank bourbon, and the Stanfields had not shared a bedroom for years.

TWENTY-THREE

THE NEWS OF HAL STANFIELD'S death filled the dining room at the club. Apparently, every member who could wanted to have lunch where it all began and marvel over what had happened. It was the same with the waitresses, all abuzz, wide-eyed and open-mouthed—can you believe it?

Noreen could believe it. She could believe anything about Mrs. Pauline Stanfield, and in a dark part of her soul she was glad that it was generally agreed she had killed her husband.

"Of course she killed him," Marge said, running a hand over the flare of her hip. She had an unbelievable figure but a face that was plain as sin. She spoke now as if she had been an eyewitness. Behind the bar, Leo concentrated on making the drinks.

"She'll get off," Noreen said.

Marge sniffed. "Of course she will."

One of Noreen's tables had only three women at it. "Mrs. Stanfield was supposed to join us," Valerie Prince whispered to Noreen. Noreen looked appropriately impressed.

"Not that *you'll* miss her," Mrs. Boswick said, leaning forward so that her pearls lay on the table. She smiled at Noreen with complicity. "The way that woman treats you!"

Noreen lifted her brows and tipped her head to one side. "The special is the crab salad."

"What did she have against you dear?" Lillian Norman's tone invited confidence.

This was as bad as anything Pauline Stanfield had ever done. Three of them quizzing her in that insinuating way. Noreen's ballpoint almost broke under the pressure of her grip, and she could not stop the blush from spreading over her cheeks.

"You'll have to ask her."

"Oh, she won't tell either."

"I'll be back to take your orders," Noreen said, and fled for the kitchen.

What a stupid way to behave. What was wrong with her? But she knew what it was. A man with whom she had had an affair was dead. Hal had not been good to her, or for her, but she felt genuinely sorry that he was dead. There had been good times with him. There would have been no more of those even if he had lived, but it didn't matter. She had some pleasant memories.

In the restroom, she dampened a paper towel with cold water and held it to her face. Those awful women. They must suspect the reason for Pauline Stanfield's behavior toward her. She had never said it, but Noreen sensed that Mrs. Stanfield knew about her and Hal. Maybe Hal had told her—it would have been like him.

A dreadful thought occurred to her. Would that come out, now that Hal was dead? Good God, imagine it in the paper—Noreen Jensen, once the girlfriend of a murdered man.

Marge looked in. "Anything wrong? Your tables are complaining."

"I don't feel well."

"We'll cover for you."

"Thanks, Marge. I can do it."

And she did. She marched into the dining room, took orders, served her tables, and got through the meal without any further difficulty. The three women who had been so prying were now occupied with speculation about the Stanfields.

"God knows how often he was unfaithful to her," Valerie Prince said in a carrying voice.

"The knowledge is not confined to God."

The three heads bent forward over the table and the gossip went on. Noreen wondered if they would know about Silvia. The thought sent her mind along another path. After she had served dessert, Noreen called and made an appointment to have her hair done. She specified that she wanted Silvia herself.

Not only was every table in the dining room taken, there was a second wave almost as plentiful, so that at two-fifteen they were still very much at it. At the bar Noreen asked Leo for two vodka martinis, a beer, and a white wine.

"Big day." It was the first thing he had said to her.

"It's like an Irish wake."

"Thanks for taking me home last night."

She smiled. "You're lucky I didn't know you lived in Privett. I would have made you walk."

"I've walked it."

"Ha, I'll bet."

"I would have had to if you hadn't given me the lift."

"You've got a nice house," she said.

She could feel his eyes on her as she walked off with the tray of drinks, and it affected the way she moved. Oh, nothing exaggerated, but a woman naturally walks differently in front of a man, especially when she thinks about it. Noreen felt she was infinitely graceful and that behind her Leo Barany was paying very careful attention.

The thought of him was the distraction she needed to get through that lunch. Not that she thought directly about him; she just let the vague memory of that drive to Privett hover on the edge of her mind, let the sound of his voice echo in her memory, and generally just let future possibilities tease her as she moved among the tables, feeling like a ballet dancer. But every time she went into the bar for drinks, he was busy with several other girls as well and nothing was said.

At three the dining room was clear, the tables had been readied for dinner and Noreen broke a rule and joined the girls who had a quickie in the lounge before using the few hours until dinner as they wished. This was when Noreen usually headed right for home, in order to be there when Karen came home from school, but today was different. Today there was the death of Hal Stanfield, and everyone was pooling what they had picked up from their tables. Leo came around the bar with a diet drink and joined them.

He didn't say anything, Noreen noticed that. He nodded, followed what everyone said, looked interested, but he had nothing to say himself, not until they tracked back to the big fight and Marge asked Leo what exactly had happened.

"I tried to stop him, grabbed his arm. They were both mad, very mad. The way he looked at *me*. Anyway, he belted her with his left hand while I was holding his right."

"Did she hit him back?"

Leo tucked in his chin and looked at Marge.

Noreen said, "She didn't have a poker then."

They nodded in silence and that pretty much wrapped it up. It was three-thirty, she could be home in fifteen minutes and have almost two hours before she had to be back. Leo came out of the cloakroom carrying her coat.

"Thanks."

"Let me give you a ride."

"I've got a car."

"Where are you going?"

"Home."

He nodded. "Too far for me."

"What do you do between lunch and dinner?"

He looked at her. "Read."

"You're a strange bartender, do you know that?"

"You have to be strange to be a bartender."

She doubted that he had to tend bar, however, so it didn't make much sense. "Come home with me," she said. "You can meet my daughter."

They went in his car—why not?—and on the way he said, "Have they talked to you yet?"

"Who?"

"The police. The sheriff. Whoever."

"About the Stanfields? I don't know anything."

"They'll talk to everybody. I figure I'll have to describe that fight until I'm really sick of it."

"I suppose. But I didn't see it."

"Oh, they'll want to know anything and everything. When people came, when they left."

"Have they talked to you yet?"

"Her lawyer did. Andrew Broom."

"I didn't see him in the dining room."

"He didn't have lunch."

The lawyer had questioned him in the bar. "I hope I didn't say too much to help her."

"What do you have against her?"

"The way she treated you."

TWENTY-FOUR

WHEN CLEARY appealed for help, they sent an investigator named Fox from Indianapolis, but before getting started on the inquiry into Hal Stanfield's murder, the sheriff had to take his lumps because of the Duff Hogan fiasco.

"What made you rule out suicide?"

"Well, Hogan confessed and the body was buried where he said."

"Covered with brush," Fox murmured, his tone suggesting that the bodies of suicides were usually found covered with brush on the banks of the Wabash.

Cleary ate crow almost cheerfully. Whatever else he might claim, he did not think of himself as a detective. He needed Fox and he was willing to beg if necessary. There was no way in the world he and Landers could build the kind of case Yoder would need, not with Andrew Broom representing Pauline Stanfield.

Fox took a room at the Ben Hur Hotel, usurped Cleary's desk when he came to the office, and listened sleepily as the sheriff gave him the details. Fox recited it back to him when Cleary was done, to make sure he had gotten it right, ticking off the points on his stubby fingers.

"So we got a stormy marriage, both spouses talking divorce for years and finally she files, they fight in public and later that night he is beaten to death with a poker in the kitchen of his home while the wife has taken refuge in the apartment of a friend. That about it?"

Fox's lower lip rolled out after he spoke and the lids of his eyes lowered.

"More or less."

"How less?"

"Mrs. Stanfield filed for divorce the morning after her husband was murdered."

"Tell me about that."

Twenty-four hours after arriving in Wyler, Fox was cautioning Yoder against bringing an indictment against Pauline Stanfield. No wonder. Already he knew more dirt about the town than Cleary had even guessed. Like the fooling around the Stanfields had done.

"She had something going with a guy named Corbett from Shipshewana. Her husband was involved with a waitress from the country club as well as a woman named Silvia Wood. Know her? She runs a chain of massage parlors."

"Tanning parlors," Cleary said.

Fox's lower lip rolled wetly out and he dipped his head to look over his glasses at Cleary. "Whatever. She was a friend of Mrs. Stanfield's too. Some town you've got here."

"I told you she spent the night with Silvia Wood."

"Are you saying her alibi is her best friend?"

Did Fox think Mrs. Stanfield would spend the night with a stranger? But it did put things in a different light.

"You got any other basis than their say-so for thinking she spent the night there?" Fox asked.

When Cleary interviewed other occupants of the building where Silvia Wood lived to see if they had noticed Mrs. Stanfield arrive that night, he found two who saw her leave in the morning. But it was Dora Arnold on the second floor who surprised Cleary.

"Not her, him. But then, he's here a lot."

The couch she sat on had a spread thrown over it and Dora seemed not to be putting her full weight of maybe 105 pounds on it. She looked as if she had not completely sat down yet or was in the process of getting up. There were throw rugs to protect the carpet and doilies on the arms of the chair in which Cleary sat. Dora was in her mid-seventies and still determined to make her furniture last a lifetime. Her brows went up when she spoke and she held her coffee mug in both hands.

"I'm talking about the night he got killed, Mrs. Arnold."

"So am I. He was here to see her."

"You're sure about that?"

"I know you'll think me a nosy old woman. Maybe I am. Maybe I'm just old-fashioned. But I don't like the idea of a kept woman living in this building. Maybe that's too strong a description. But Harold Stanfield was here a lot, skulking in and out. He hasn't changed a bit since I had him as a third-grader."

"You taught Stanfield?"

"He was in my class at Booth Tarkington, yes."

"You saw him here the night of August sixteenth?"

After a moment she nodded solemnly. "When he left."

"What time was that?"

"'Late Night with David Letterman' was on. It was after eleven."

"Mrs. Stanfield spent that night with Silvia Wood."

"I don't know anything about that."

"You're certain it was the night he was killed that Harold Stanfield was here?"

"Sheriff, when I heard the news the following day, I realized that the last time I had seen him alive was when I looked out that window and watched him get into his car and drive away the night before."

"How did you know he was visiting Silvia Wood?"

"That was an inference, based on his past habits."

"Meaning he often came here to see her."

"And he knew I knew he was up to no good. Once I confronted him in the hallway and asked in a very pointed way how his wife was. Of course, he owns this building. That was his excuse for being here."

Cleary told Fox of the two tenants who had seen Pauline Stanfield leave the following morning, but he held back on Dora's claim. First he wanted to ask Silvia Wood about it.

"I WAS A GOOD FRIEND of both the Stanfields," Silvia said when Cleary talked with her in the office of what she called her flagship, the first tanning parlor she had opened in Wyler.

"He visited you at your apartment."

"So did she."

"I meant alone."

"They both did."

"Were they together when they visited you the night Harold Stanfield was killed?"

If he ever ran away with another woman, Cleary hoped it would be someone like Silvia Wood. She was not a woman you were likely to think of as a wife or mother. Her manner spelled excitement or trouble, depending on your point of view. Silvia Wood belonged to an entirely different species from Mrs. Cleary, no doubt about that. Maybe it was the speculative way she was looking at him that brought on these thoughts.

"It would be a lot easier if I could tell you things in confidence, Sheriff Cleary."

"What sort of things?"

"I am a woman of flesh and blood."

"I never doubted it."

"You're a good man, Sheriff. A solid man. You might have harassed me because of my business, given what some people said, but you never did, and I appreciate it. I think you knew my tanning parlors were only what they claimed to be. The bankers of this town didn't believe that. The only reason they loaned me money was because Hal Stanfield became my silent partner. You didn't know that, did you?"

"No, I didn't."

"Our relations were not confined to business."

Cleary said nothing, trying not to blink, trying not to swallow. He might have known that Stanfield would make a play for her, however startling it was to have the hunch corroborated by the woman involved. What really surprised him was to learn that Silvia and Stanfield had been business partners.

"He invested in your parlors?"

"Did you understand what I said, Sheriff?"

"That Stanfield was your lover? I got that impression talking with Dora Arnold, who lives in the same building you do. She saw Stanfield leave your apartment the night he was killed. What time would that have been?"

"I think about eleven." She hadn't even hesitated, and Cleary had the sudden feeling they were having a conversation for which she had been preparing herself.

"Why didn't you mention this before?"

Silvia lit a cigarette. How good the smoke smelled. "Why would I have, Sheriff? You can imagine how I felt the next day when I learned he had gone home and been brutally murdered. But the fact that he had stopped by after his fight with Pauline had nothing to do with that."

"Did you tell Mrs. Stanfield?"

"She came after Hal left."

"Could I have one of your cigarettes?"

Cleary asked for a piece of paper too, so he could get things written down and make sure he had it straight. The night of August 16, Hal Stanfield had arrived at Silvia Wood's apartment after the fight at the club.

"When I visited Pauline at her house that afternoon, we had a long talk. I knew they were having trouble, but they had been having trouble ever since I met them. I suppose most married couples do."

"The Stanfields weren't like most married couples."

"Because of their money? I suppose you're right."

"What time did he get here last night?"

Cleary wrote out the schedule right there in her office, using her desktop. The fight at the club had taken place around nine and Pauline had left shortly afterward with the Brooms. He left maybe fifteen minutes after she had. At ten he arrived at Silvia Wood's.

"I'm guessing at the time. Hal came to tell me all about the fight. That's no time to talk with a husband, right after he's had a fight with his wife. Especially a husband with whom you're having an affair. I urged him to go home to Pauline. And that is what he did. Leaving at about eleven."

"That's the time you said Pauline got here."

"Did I?"

"Do you want to correct that?"

"All I know, Sheriff, is that I marveled that they hadn't run into one another coming and going. If only they had."

"Mrs. Stanfield says that after she left the country club she just drove around."

"She was understandably upset. I suppose it's because we'd had our talk that afternoon that she decided to come here."

"Did you tell her that her husband had been here?"

"No, I didn't. Nor did I tell her to go home. At the time that seemed the right thing to do, or not to do. Maybe I saved her life."

"Maybe."

Intriguing as it might be, Cleary was not sure what it meant that both the Stanfields had gone to Silvia Wood that night. But it gave him something Fox did not know and, important or not, he felt good about that. The inspector from Indianapolis was no one you'd want to get stuck on a desert island with. He seemed to spend an awful lot of time in the Roundball Lounge, and it was Landers who guessed that the inspector's information about the town came from Healy of the *Wyler Dealer*. Just because it wasn't news fit to print didn't mean the reporter couldn't broadcast it over drinks. Cleary lost respect for Fox then, and his confidence in his own investigative abilities returned. Anybody could have made a mistake about Larry Moss.

NOREEN REFUSED to talk to him, at first because she was busy, later on principle. Cleary tried to catch her in the bar of the club, but it was lunchtime and she couldn't spare a minute, so the sheriff sat at the bar and watched the waitresses come and go, fetching drinks for the diners. The man behind the bar performed his job efficiently, making drinks appear in a wink, but even when he wasn't busy, he kept busy, and always at the far end of the bar, away from Cleary.

"How long you worked here?" Cleary asked.

The bartender actually looked at his watch. "I came on at eleven."

"How long you been bartender here?"

"Couple months."

"Do you live in Wyler?"

"Did your assistant lose his notes, or don't you share information?"

Touchy sonofabitch, Cleary was only making conversation. He would like to know what the guy knew about Stanfield and the waitress Noreen. What was the bartender's name. Brown? Brain? He got off the stool and went to Harrison's office. The manager of the club was cooperative, if only in the hope that he could get the sheriff out of the place as soon as possible.

"What's the bartender's name?"

"Leo Barany."

"How long he worked for you?"

"I hired him in May."

"Where's he from?"

"Privett."

Cleary went back to the bar. "Barany," he called after he got settled again. "Tell me something."

"Sure."

"Where did you work in Privett before you came here?"

"Wouldn't Harrison tell you?"

Just like that—didn't even look at the sheriff when he asked. "You don't miss much do you?"

Barany shrugged.

"What can you tell me about Stanfield and hanky-panky with the help?"

Barany looked at him. Large cold eyes. "He never made a pass at me."

"A waitress?"

"Which one?"

"Noreen Jensen."

Barany made a face. "I don't know anything about it."

"It could have been before your time."

"What do you mean?"

The eyes were no longer cold but sparking with anger. Even with that ridiculous jacket and his essentially silly job, Barany retained his dignity. In Cleary's experience bartenders were usually even more eager to talk than managers. Maybe they secretly hoped something they said would cause their boss trouble.

"Forget it. Give me another beer."

The glass was scarcely three-quarters full, but Cleary didn't mind. He had never liked the taste of beer, and liquor was worse. The waitresses had a couple of hours between the noon and evening meals and Harrison had told him most of them took off. Noreen's unwillingness to talk made him more determined to ask her about her relationship with Stanfield. All he was doing here was being ignored by the bartender and watching the girls' brisk arrivals and departures. Barany treated her no differently than he did the other girls, so either he already knew of her connection with Stanfield or it meant nothing to him. Cleary left his unfinished beer, went downstairs and through the golf shop to the parking lot, where he settled into the unmarked car and almost immediately wished he had stopped by the john on his way out. Rule One for a stakeout was to get comfortable first. There must be a restroom near the golf shop, but he was afraid he would lose his advantage if he went back into the club now. Barany had watched him go to Harrison's office, but there was no way in the world that, from the bar, he could see the parking lot.

He chewed some Big Red, listened to the radio, tried by sliding down in the seat to relieve the pressure on his bladder, jiggled his foot, and irrationally blamed his discomfort on that sonofabitch of a bartender. It was difficult to retain the conviction that sitting here in a sweltering parking lot made a lot of sense. He could just as easily wait for Noreen at the home address Harrison had provided him. It was her habit to leave between the midday and evening meals, and Harrison thought she went home. But what if she didn't? He would rather follow her from the club and make sure he could pin her down.

It was an hour later when she came out. She was not alone. Barany the bartender was with her. Dammit! No doubt he would tell her the sheriff was asking about her fooling around with Stanfield. He should have kept his mouth shut, but at the time it seemed a way to get the bartender talking.

The waitress was a more attractive example of her sex than Barany was of his, but then Cleary could never figure out what made men attractive to women. Barany opened the passenger door for her, and his step seemed light when he rounded the car and got in behind the wheel.

Cleary followed them because the alternative was to admit that he had wasted several hours.

TWENTY-FIVE

IT HAD BEEN NINE DAYS since he killed Hal Stanfield and there were times when Barany was sure it hadn't happened. Were his parents and Slattery the silver-tongued really buried beneath the concrete floor of the sheet-metal shed behind the house on Wabash Road?

He had to think a bit to remember how long it had been since he killed the old man. Late April, a rainy night, rain had fallen all day, washing away an unseasonably late snow, a Saturday. There was a golf match on television, and each time Leo brought his father a beer, he laced it with a stronger dose of arsenic. Then he carried him through the rain to the shed, thinking up the story he would tell Ma when she got home. Only she was already home and at the kitchen window watching him carry the old man to the shed. She looked gray and depressed, maybe the doctor had given her bad news; but even if he hadn't, it seemed more an act of mercy than anything else when Leo looped the cord of her iron over her head and let it slip down to her throat. She had been a tough, proud woman, but it had taken maybe two minutes to choke the life out of her. He often thought of that afterward. Every living thing is only a few ticks of the clock away from nothingness.

He left his parents lying on the dirt floor of the shed that night and throughout Sunday. On Monday the rain stopped and he dug their grave, maybe four feet deep, taking away the surplus dirt from the shed in the wheelbarrow and dumping it in his father's garden. He threw the arsenic in after them before shoveling dirt over them.

Later, when he made a hole for Slattery, he was afraid the shovel would strike the bodies of his parents, so he dug well off to one side. That had been in June—June 14, Flag Day. He remembered because Slattery had called him up and pretended to be selling American flags for display on this special day. Barany hung up, drove to Slattery's and pressed the door button. He had been by the house more than once, wanting to get a glimpse of his tormentor. Apparently, Slattery had not bothered to find out what Leo Barany looked like. He let Leo in, falling for the story that his car had broken down and he wanted to call the AAA.

He had enjoyed killing Slattery. He tied his hands and feet and slowly stuffed a very large flag down his throat. Well, most of it. When Slattery finally choked to death, there was still a lot of flag hanging out of his mouth. After dark, Barany wrapped the body in a sheet, put it in the trunk of his car, and drove it slowly home for burial in the sheet-metal shed. Three days later he laid the concrete floor of the shed, something he regretted when he decided that Pauline Stanfield would have to join the others—his parents and Slattery.

As he thought of it now, disposing of her body seemed unnecessary. No one would connect him with her in any way. The murder would have no explanation. There would be no theft, no rape, nothing to indicate why she had been killed. It would be as inexplicable as what insurance companies call an Act of God.

The sheriff hanging around the bar during the noontime rush, asking Harrison his name, making cracks about Noreen and Stanfield, got to Barany, and when he and Noreen drove off on their afternoon break, he had forgotten all about his promise to show her the house.

"Leo, you're the one who brought it up."

"It's just a house."

But he could see the disappointment in her face. Her beauty was not an indoor thing. She was even prettier in the sunlight. He found it easy to believe that Stanfield had been attracted to her. He assured her they would go look at his house.

"A promise is a promise," he said.

"Look, if you'd rather not, Leo."

Now she wanted him to beg her to come see the damned house. "You should have talked with the sheriff, Noreen. Sooner or later you'll have to. You might just as well get it over with."

"I've already told them all I know, which is nothing. I wish they would just leave me alone."

"Who's talked with you?"

"The worst one was Fox."

"Cleary asked me if I had ever heard of anything going on between you and Stanfield."

She made an angry sound. "Fox actually asked me if I had killed Hal."

Hal? "What did you tell him?"

"Don't be funny."

"Who dropped whom?"

She glared at him. "You're as bad as they are."

He let it go, but he felt as if he had been kicked in the chest. Which was ridiculous. Noreen wasn't a virgin, she had a daughter almost in her teens, and as far as he knew, it was his house she liked, not him. Before she saw the house, she had paid no attention to Leo Barany. Well, he had seen her place and he couldn't blame her.

Coming up the drive from the Wabash Road, he tried to see the house as she must be seeing it. That meant not seeing it as the trilevel atrocity his father had substituted for the stately frame house in which his mother had been raised. Unlocking the front door, it dawned on him that he had brought a beautiful woman home and the two of them would be alone in the house. The thought made him more nervous than anything else.

At thirty-four Leo Barany's knowledge of women was confined to pornographic movies and purchased sex. The porn made him feel like a kid, and the sex made him feel as if he had just bought a lemon off a used car lot. Whenever he tried to imagine a man and a woman loving one another, memories of his parents got in the way. It took an act of faith to think of the two of them in the sack together. But even that was easier than imagining himself in bed with Noreen.

Inside the house she wandered through the rooms, oohing and ahhing, and Leo thought how pleased his father would have been, maybe his mother too—she had worked as hard as the old man to make it a pleasant place. They ended up in the breezeway, drinking iced tea, and he told her the story of the Deveres and the Depression and all that lost land.

"The land the Walnut Grove Golf Course is on was ours."

"When did your parents pass away?" She said it as if she were addressing a mourner at a funeral.

"That's hard to say."

She gave him a puzzled look.

"Officially, they're just missing. I can't inherit anything for five years. That's why I'm tending bar."

"But how can they just be missing?"

"They went to Florida at Easter time and never came back."

"Just this past Easter?"

"That's right."

"But Leo, they could walk in here any minute."

Her expression told him he was not acting the way someone whose parents had vanished into thin air ought to act. He frowned and looked out across the lawn, his eyes avoiding the sheet-metal shed.

"I've learned not to hope," he said.

She got up and came to stand beside his chair. He felt her hand soft on his shoulder, and before he knew it, he was crying, bawling like a kid, and she knelt beside his chair and put her arm around him, and he buried his face in her beautiful hair and went on crying. It was the unaccustomed feel of her hand that had done it. Tenderness, compassion, a feeling binding people together. He had no practice with any of that and she had caught him unawares. When she began to pat him on the back, he got over it. He stood and blinked away the tears.

"It's the first time I cried for them," he said, and this time he did look at the shed. He wasn't sorry they were dead, but it was sad.

After a decent interval they got back to the fact that he had to wait before anything was legally his. Noreen asked who his lawyer was and just shook her head at the mention of the name.

"You should consult Andrew Broom, Leo. I'll bet he could find a way around the technicalities."

"He'll be pretty busy defending Pauline Stanfield."

"Ha! It'll be a cold day in hell when they accuse her of anything."

"Maybe you're right."

"You know I am."

It was still too soon to say Pauline was off the hook, but Leo did not like the delay. Obviously, no one else knew she had been in the house when her husband was killed. The thought that he had accidentally made a billiard shot, killing her husband and then having the state kill her as a murderer, no longer made a lot of sense. In the first place, there was no way in the world she would ever spend the rest of her life in prison if she was found guilty. Second, Noreen's high estimate of Andrew Broom merely echoed the general opinion. Getting Hogan off looked easy after the fact, but beforehand people had been sure Broom was heading for defeat. Pauline's story of driving around before going to Silvia Wood's to spend the night sounded fishy, but Leo could believe Broom would convince a jury she really had been aimlessly driving around Wyler at the time her husband was killed.

"She's lucky to have someone back up her story that she spent the night with Silvia Wood."

"People saw her leave there in the morning."

"But when did she get there?"

"I don't think it matters," Noreen said. "Nobody really thinks she could have killed her husband."

"Why not?"

She sat down again and took a sip of her iced tea. She shook her head. "I just can't imagine her doing it."

"Can you imagine yourself killing anyone?"

"No!"

"Oh, come on. Didn't you ever fight with your husband and get so mad you wished he was dead? Did you ever strike him, throw something…" Her eyes filled with memories and she looked away. Leo said softly, "Well, Pauline Stanfield has a lot worse temper than you'll ever have."

It didn't convince her and he let it go. What he had done was convince himself that Pauline Stanfield was in no danger of being tried or convicted.

After ten days of thinking he was off the hook, Barany realized he was right back where he had been on August 16. Pauline Stanfield had to die and it was up to him to see that she did.

She was still living in a suite in the Ben Hur Hotel, on record as saying that she would sell the house in which Hal was murdered, certainly never live there again herself, far more a grieving widow than a murder suspect.

That night after work Barany drove home, packed a suitcase, and returned to Wyler, where he checked in at the Ben Hur using the name of one of his old professors in Minneapolis.

The Ben Hur occupied the top six floors of the First Bank Building, no place for anyone with a fear of fire, and Pauline Stanfield's suite was on the top floor, which also had meeting rooms and a lounge called the Eye in the Sky. Barany lay on the bed in his room and looked at the stippled ceiling. A smoke alarm hung there like a creature from outer space. How vulnerable the hotel was, with five floors intervening between it and ground level, accessible only by elevator, with the emergency stairways running past vaultlike doors on the bank floors. That night Barany acquainted himself with the layout, much as he had prowled the Stanfield house for weeks in advance of the big night.

He felt as though he was going back into training.

TWENTY-SIX

PAULINE WAS BORED. Bored with the Ben Hur Hotel, bored with being expected to act like a widow, bored with Andrew Broom and the constant sessions meant to prepare her for a trial that nobody else thought was going to take place. Every time they talked, Pauline was afraid she would say something that would tell him she was lying about how she had spent the time before going to Silvia's.

What difference did it make anyway? No one seriously thought she had killed Hal. She had fled the house as much out of terror as fear of being thought guilty. Who would find it suspicious that a woman ran from the house in which her husband had just been brutally murdered? But she did not want to tell Andrew she had lied.

So talking with him was torture. As if the whole thing was a lie. Finally, she told Silvia, to relieve the pressure, so someone else would know. It hadn't helped.

"You were in the house when it happened!" Silvia was pop-eyed with surprise.

"Upstairs. I had no idea what was going on. I must have been in the shower."

It all came tumbling out, and then Silvia got started with her questions and it was almost as bad as with Andrew. Trying to regain the flavor of their earlier conversations, Pauline admitted that what had brought her rushing downstairs was the fear that Hal was emptying the safe of her valuables.

"The sound of the phone off the hook made me go into the kitchen and that's when I found him."

"But who killed him?"

"I don't know! But it must have happened just before I came downstairs. Silvia, imagine! I might have run right into the killer."

"You have to tell Andrew Broom."

"What for? It's silly to think anyone will accuse me of killing Hal."

"All the more reason to tell him."

"Maybe I will."

By the time Silvia realized Pauline was telling her all this because she wanted sympathy, it was too late. Pauline wished she had kept her mouth shut. Or, if she had to tell someone, she wished she had told Andrew Broom. At least he had a professional obligation to keep it a secret, whereas Silvia... She decided she *would* tell Andrew, if only to make sure he would hear it from her directly.

She and Silvia had been having a drink together in her suite at the Ben Hur. Although the thought of going home filled her with distaste, it was nonetheless true that she was staying in this hotel at the suggestion of Andrew. He wanted her to stay out of sight and talk to no one, but he could hardly expect her to just disappear from the face of the earth. He had even been reluctant to say she could phone Silvia and have her come to the hotel.

"You're bound to tell her things you shouldn't."

"Andrew, she may be my best friend."

He looked surprised. "How long have you known her?"

"It doesn't take long to know some people well."

"Only Hal was her business partner, wasn't he?"

"What do you mean?"

"Did you put any money into Silvia Wood's business?"

"None of my own," Pauline said carefully.

"Well, you'll be her silent partner after probate. Because of Hal's investment."

She was too proud to show that this was news to her. Hal and Silvia in business together, and after what he had said about the tanning parlors? What a hypocrite he had been. And how closemouthed Silvia was. The thought of this secret between her husband and Silvia gave Pauline something to think about there in her suite at the Ben Hur. Had more than business been involved? It was an intriguing thought, not least because she could not say what exactly her feeling would be if it were true.

The afternoon she revealed to Silvia that she had been in the house when Hal was killed, peeved at the lack of immediate sympathy, she had suggested that Silvia was pretty good at keeping secrets herself.

"If you're worried I'll tell anyone this, don't be."

"I was thinking of the money Hal put into your business."

"But that's no secret."

"You never mentioned it before."

"But neither did you. I assumed you didn't want to talk about my business."

Silvia's reaction made it impossible for Pauline to admit that Hal had not told her of the investment.

"Tell me something, Silvia. Did Hal ever make a move on you?"

"Of course."

"Well?"

Silvia's eyes met hers directly and nothing in them told Pauline a thing. "You know the answer to that, Pauline.

I think he did too. I suppose he had to get rid of that possibility before we could have a business relationship.''

To pursue this would have put Pauline at more of a disadvantage than asking for details of Hal's investment in Silvia's business. She had wanted them to have another drink before Silvia left—they had only had two—but now she wanted to be alone. As if she had a choice. It dawned on her that she was very much alone now, and the realization brought on a delicious sadness she wanted to enjoy in solitude.

Susannah Broom called to invite her to dinner, but Pauline said no. The invitation was obviously prompted by pity or compassion or some motive Pauline did not want to encourage. After she hung up, Pauline smoked and sipped her drink and felt sorry for herself. She was both an orphan and a widow now.

Within an hour she was sorry she had not accepted the invitation to dine with the Brooms. She had half a mind to drive to the club or maybe up to South Bend, but the thoughts hardly formulated in her mind before she rejected them. For one thing, she was in no condition to drive. Hadn't she read somewhere that eventually prisoners begin to love their cells, dreading to leave them, wanting the confinement that at first threatened to drive them mad? It was fanciful to think of her suite as a cell, but Pauline found the prospect of spending yet another evening here, calling room service, watching television, far from repellent. It was the essence of boredom and she was beginning to love it.

Half an hour later, changed, freshened up, she left her suite and went to the Eye in the Sky. Two windowed walls revealed the twinkling lights of Wyler; the recessed lighting set in a glittering ceiling barely illumined the room in which silhouetted figures leaned toward one another across small tables. There were the inevitable loud voices and laughter from the bar, which by contrast seemed brightly lit. Pauline moved toward it through the tables, exhilarated by the attention she commanded. The faces at the bar were the faces of strangers. She had the sudden conviction that no one here would know who she was. It would be an anonymous evening and the prospect excited her.

She made sure of that by lying about herself when the professor from Minneapolis took the stool next to hers, telling him she was from Chicago, just passing through.

"What brings a professor to Wyler, Indiana?" she asked, watching herself in the mirror behind the bar. The light was kind, even flattering, and she liked her languid look as she asked the question.

"Does the name Edgar Rice Burroughs mean anything to you?"

"Should it?"

"Yes, but I'm not surprised it doesn't. He was the creator of Tarzan."

Burroughs had traveled out of Chicago as a young man before his fiction had made him wealthy, and Professor Lynch ("Call me Bernie") was making a meticulous record of those business trips, which had taken place in the twenties. Pauline could not imagine what interest such information could hold, but Bernie seemed a nice combination of academic otherworldliness and, well, worldliness. She liked the way he bought her next drink without making a fuss about it. They might have been talking together at a faculty party.

That is how she began to think of it. She had given her name as Pauline Halton, her mother's maiden name, telling him she was en route to Louisville to see her sister.

"Married?"

The stranger she had become considered the question in the mirror behind the bar, looking back at herself from among the real and reflected bottles. "Not anymore."

"Ah."

"You?"

"I'm not the marrying kind."

They seemed to toast their status. She liked him. He reminded her vaguely of someone she knew, and it seemed a stroke of luck to have a professor sit down beside her. The chances were far greater that it would be a salesman, some pushy type who would want to explain computers to her and assume that he would be going to her room afterward. Bernie was easy to talk with, making all the trivia he knew about the creator of Tarzan so interesting, she urged him to go on. She would bet he was a much-sought-after dinner guest. When he asked about her, it was clear he would not mind if she chose not to tell him much about herself, and this made her all the more eager to do so—of her fictional self, that is. It would have been easier if she had not lied to him, but she could scarcely enjoy this if she told him her husband had been killed just a few days ago. And much of the fun of the evening was being someone else.

On the second drink they shared, they moved to a table, and that was even nicer. It was easier to lie when she couldn't see her reflected self doing it. He drew his chair close to her because it was getting noisier in the bar. People were grouped around the piano, singing golden oldies with uncertain voices. The volume increased gradually until she had to put her ear next to Bernie's mouth to hear what he was saying.

"This is impossible," he said, frowning at the singers, but with a begrudging smile too.

"We could go to my suite."

He turned his wrist until the face of his watch was illumined by an overhead light. "Why not? You're awfully easy to talk to."

It seemed the nicest thing anyone had ever said to her. As they were leaving the bar, she was suddenly reminded of the lounge at the club, of being struck by Hal and staggering back into the darkness to fall among the tables. She put her arm through Bernie's. She would show Hal.

TWENTY-SEVEN

JUST LET IT HAPPEN. That had been Leo's policy from
the beginning, and if the results had not been good on
August 16, the method seemed more promising now.
What luck to find her sitting at the bar in the Eye in the
Sky, an empty stool beside her. He did not worry that she
might recognize him. Few members took much notice of
the help, looking at them maybe, but not really seeing
them. This was triply true of Mrs. Stanfield. If he had
ever questioned the wisdom of registering as Professor
Bernard Lynch from Minneapolis, his doubts would have
fled when he watched her reaction to his supposed
professional status. It was a role he had coveted for so
long, and now, at least for the moment, it was his, and he
played it to perfection.

But the completely unlooked-for bonus was her lying
about herself and using the name Halton. It was her
Grandfather Halton who had foreclosed on his Grandfather Devere. *"Memento mori,"* he said when she raised
the first drink he bought her in a toast.

"What does that mean?"

"It's Yale's motto."

"You went to Yale?"

He nodded. "For my doctorate. I did undergraduate
work at Notre Dame."

Most of the stuff he told her about Burroughs he made
up, but not all. He had taken a course in popular culture
devoted to the *oeuvres* of Max Brand, Zane Grey, and
Edgar Rice Burroughs. It was the kind of trivia that got

one through academic parties. Barany liked it because it seemed a parody of scholarship. Who are we to say that Burroughs is any less important than Howells? That was the unprincipled question of the course. He told Pauline Stanfield, aka Halton, that they were living in the twilight of civilization. She loved it. He told her he was writing a book called *Civilization and Its Discontents*. He had to repeat it, speaking directly into her ear, and then she suggested they adjourn to her suite. Let it happen.

In the dim light of the bar, she might have been any age, but in the hallway and in her room she was an unquestionable forty-one. She seemed to be waiting for his reaction to the fact that she had ten years on him, but he asked where the john was and that relaxed her. The bathroom was so bright it hurt his eyes. He put his hands on the basin and leaned forward, his nose almost touching the mirror, looking deep into the eyes of a man about to kill a woman.

Execute a woman, he corrected. *And what is the charge?* Charges, Your Honor. Unforgivable rudeness when presented with the opportunity of a lifetime in magazine subscriptions. Not just lack of interest, not pique at being half-conned, but rage that such vermin as himself should have the temerity to telephone her. *You said "charges."* Yes, Your Honor. The accused is the offspring of the infamous Halton who foreclosed on Grandpa Devere's mortgage. All the accumulated discontent taught him by his mother seethed now in Leo Barany. Pauline Stanfield had to die.

How? Keep it simple. The bathroom was plentifully supplied with towels, several shower towels four feet long. He pulled back the sliding door and looked into the shower. A small metallic square caught his eye. There was another opposite it. It proved to be a clothesline. Barany smiled. Provision for rinsing out a few things in the luxury suite of the Ben Hur. He let go of the line and it snapped back into the wall.

Only two lamps burned when he came back to the sitting room. She was examining the contents of the little refrigerator.

"If you want scotch, I'll have to send for some. All I have left is bourbon."

"Bourbon is fine." They had been seen together in the bar, perhaps noticed leaving together, but he did not want a boy from room service actually to see him in the suite with her. There were four miniature bottles of bourbon and she divided them equally. It was now obvious to Barany that she had already drunk too much. A mixed blessing. She would be easier to handle, but he wanted her to know why this was happening to her.

They sat together on a two-cushion couch, and she leaned her head on his shoulder and sighed. She raised her glass a few inches. "Here's to Tarzan and Wyler, Indiana."

"Me Tarzan, you Jane."

She actually giggled.

So letting it happen took him down an unintended path. That he should make love to a woman he hated and meant to kill would have seemed, before the fact, impossible, but there in the suite with Pauline Stanfield already far gone in drink, it seemed fated. She turned her face up to his and he kissed her, tentatively, and then she was grinding her lips to his and twisting in his arms so that her plush breasts were pressing against him. The last woman he had made love to was a drunken Indian in a seedy hotel in Minneapolis, and that was six months ago. Thinking of Pauline Stanfield as a whore helped Leo perform when, after some minutes of almost painful kissing on the couch, she had rolled free, taken his hand, and led him into the bedroom.

"I snore," she said in a playful warning afterward.

The fact that he had truly enjoyed what they had done seemed another charge against her. He threw back the sheet.

"Where are you going?"

"Let's shower."

She had been ready to drop off, but the fear that he would just go jolted her and now the suggestion that they shower brought a crooked smile to her lips. She slid out of bed and once more took his hand.

In the bathroom, while he adjusted the water, he looked up at the metal knob of the clothesline. He stepped into the water and she followed, squealing as she entered the spray, backing against him, lifting her face to the water. Leo slid his hands down her sides, over the flare of her hips, and moved her forward into the stinging water.

He reached back with one hand and grasped the stainless-steel ball and pulled. The thin line must have been six feet long. Leo needed both hands to bring it over her head and down to her throat.

"What are you doing?"

"Relax, Pauline. You are about to die and I want you to know why."

She began to struggle then, her elbow digging into his chest, her eyes looking wildly over her shoulder. He let her turn, the line sliding around her neck as she did. When she looked up at him, her hair soggy and fallen, her eyes filled with every fear she had ever known.

"Who are you?"

"I'm calling to tell you that you have won a prize."

She searched his eyes. She didn't remember. Did it matter?

"You killed Hal," she whispered. Her hands had risen to her throat and were trying to loosen the clothesline.

"That's right."

"Why?"

"I was there to kill you."

Suddenly, pain shot through him and he bent forward and backed away. The bitch had kneed him. He thought he was going to throw up. Now she was reaching for him, and he made a great parenthesis of his body to keep out of her reach—and tightened the line around her neck. She lost her footing and pulled him down into the tub, the shower beating on the back of his head. That was when the clothesline snapped.

A great noise issued from her as the pressure let up and she squirmed out from under him and pulled the shower curtain over his head. By the time he got free of it, she was at the door of the bathroom. He lunged at her and grabbed the door, but his momentum added to her pulling and his fingers were caught. He bellowed in pain, all sense of caution gone now.

Clasping his hands, doubled over, he stumbled naked into the bedroom. She was beside the bed and had the phone at her ear. Barany literally dove across the bed. She turned away with the instrument in her hand, but it was the line he was after. He pulled it from the wall. She turned with the dead phone in her hands, frightened, angry, slightly ridiculous in the nude. She lifted the phone and hurled it at him.

He twisted out of the way and instinctively covered his privates. She had found his Achilles heel and might return to it. He caught up with her as she tried to go back into the bathroom, and pushed her inside and slammed the door. He wanted to think.

Immediately, he pulled the bathroom door open again. There was another phone in there and she had picked it up. Leo wrested it from her and returned it to its cradle. She was looking around desperately. The broken clothesline was in the tub where the shower still ran. Towels. Leo took one of the long ones and immediately relaxed. He smiled at Pauline.

"You are going to die."

"Leave me alone." She began to cringe, moving away, toward the door. His fingers burned and the pain in his genitals still sickened him, but he accepted that. No pain, no gain. He was twirling the towel like a jump rope when she opened the door. He did not try to stop her, but followed her into the bedroom. She snatched up her robe and ran on into the sitting room. He caught her there, near the couch where they had exchanged such passionate kisses. He caught her wrist, pushed her over the back of the couch, tipping it, but rode it to the floor with her beneath him, getting the towel around her throat and beginning to twist.

It took nearly a quarter of an hour, and the towel was no good at all. Finally, he used his bare hands, pressing his thumbs relentlessly down as she kicked and squirmed and did not easily let go her grip on life. Even when he was certain she was dead, he carried her into the bathroom, filled the tub, and submerged her in the water.

The glass he had drunk from was still half full, and he righted the couch, sat on it, and, still naked, finished the bourbon. It had been a very long time since he had drunk so much. Tending bar would cure anyone of the desire to drink. He began to shiver. His fingers were beginning to swell and his genitals ached terribly.

He could leave the body here or take it with him. Either way he was in more danger than he planned, but if she were found dead in her room, he would be the prime suspect. If she simply disappeared, as his parents and Slattery had, it would be a very different matter. Tomorrow he would show up at the club, work as usual, maybe go somewhere with Noreen afterward, and the police would maybe be checking out Professor Bernard Lynch of Minneapolis.

Leaving the body was out.

He dressed and went to his own room. All he had brought with him when he checked into the hotel was an attaché case and a small shoulder bag. He rumpled the bed to make it look slept in, and messed up the bathroom a bit, unwrapping some soap, running the water in the shower, unfolding a towel and throwing it over the shower curtain.

At one o'clock he went back to the suite, letting himself in with the key he had taken from her purse. There was money in the purse, but he wasn't interested in that. He left his things in the suite when, at two, he retraced his steps to his own room, taking the stairway. He met no one. After he went back to the suite, he took a garment bag from the closet and laid it out on the bed. In the bathroom, he let the water drain from the tub, rolled the body back and forth to get most of the water off, then picked it up and carried it to the bed. He unzipped the garment bag and rolled the body into it, lifting her knees and turning her sideways and managing to zip the thing up again. He did not relish the thought of lugging her down to his car.

TWENTY-EIGHT

GERALD ROWAN went right on up to the suite as he always did. At first this had been a precaution of sorts, since Pauline was then hiding out in the Ben Hur, but she had stayed on after her whereabouts became public knowledge, so now it was only habit. And a habit that would soon be a memory. Having parked in the basement garage, he took the express elevator to the hotel lobby, where he transferred to another car that took him to the top of the building.

Whatever the hell Andrew was up to was a mystery to Gerald. He persisted in treating Pauline as a prime suspect in her husband's murder, but everything they knew bore out her story. Fox had gone back to Indianapolis and Cleary certainly was no threat. The sheriff had tried to keep Fox in town with the revelation that Hal Stanfield had visited Silvia before going home to be killed, but the little man from Indianapolis blinked at him for a moment, then said, "I know."

"That means both Stanfields were there," Cleary said.

They were meeting in Andrew Broom's office—Gerald, the sheriff, Fox, and Andrew.

"Tell us about it." This was news to Andrew Broom, but he was not going to let vanity prevent his learning all that he could about the night of August 16. Gerald jotted down the presumed times—Fox and Cleary were in agreement—and looked at his uncle.

"Some people gave you the same time for his departure and for her arrival."

"That's right, Mr. Broom," Fox said. "Wherever your client was prior to that no longer matters. That is why I am going home."

"We still have a murder here," Cleary said.

"Yes, you do," Fox agreed. "But I don't. My instructions were limited to the possibility that Mrs. Stanfield was guilty. Is there anything else you haven't mentioned?"

Cleary actually gave him the finger and Gerald could not repress a laugh. Fox seemed to ignore the obscene gesture, shook Andrew's hand, then Gerald's, and stopped in front of Cleary.

"Better get that finger fixed, Sheriff."

"So that's that," Gerald said when he and his uncle were alone.

"How do you mean?"

"Pauline didn't do it."

"As Cleary said, we still have a murder."

"We?"

"Hal Stanfield was my client. And as for Pauline, she's been lying. Why?"

"About driving around? As Fox said, it doesn't matter what she was doing."

"It matters to me. And we know she was."

"Do we?"

"She was at home. Her shower had been used and there was a glass of bourbon on the table beside her bed. Hal never drank bourbon. Hal did not sleep in that room. She was home, about to go to bed, then got up and went to Silvia's."

"Where she nearly ran into Hal on his way out."

"I want to talk to her, Gerald."

"To tell her she's been lying?"

Andrew pulled at his upper lip with thumb and fore-finger and looked out at Wyler below his windows. Then he smiled at Gerald.

"To give her the good news."

"That she's innocent?"

"Well, that everyone thinks so but me."

The DO NOT DISTURB sign still hung on the door al-though it was fifteen minutes short of noon. That was the first oddity. Pauline didn't really get dressed until lunch-time, but Gerald had never seen that sign hung out be-fore. There was no answer to his knock. It didn't matter. The door was not locked. Gerald pushed it open and called in.

"Mrs. Stanfield? Gerald Rowan. Are you decent?"

No answer. What *was* the answer to that stupid ques-tion? Gerald went into the sitting room and stood listen-ing. What he heard was nothing—no television, no sound of water running, no sound of Pauline on the phone—and that was odd.

"Pauline?"

He called out before going into the bedroom. By the look of the bed, she had had a bad dream or had not spent the night alone. The bathroom door was ajar. She wasn't in there either.

Do not disturb? An empty room and an unlocked door. More puzzling still was the condition of the bed. A purse lay on the floor beside the night table. Gerald checked the closet and found it full of clothes. Why did he feel so strongly that Pauline had left?

He picked up the phone to call Andrew and found that it was dead. The wire had been pulled from the wall. He made the call in the sitting room.

"Stay there. I'll bring Cleary."

But when Andrew came, it was not Cleary with him but the manager, Biersma, a very large man who seemed to have been given the wrong face. Gerald followed the two men around as they made the same discoveries he had. The purse and the bedroom phone were the puzzlers.

"The clothesline in the bathroom is broken too," Biersma said in a soprano voice. It went with the twelve-year-old face if not the wrestler's body.

"Clothesline?"

Biersma brought it to Andrew, who ran it through his fingers and frowned at Gerald.

"Find out when she was last seen by anyone in the hotel."

An hour and twenty minutes later they had established that no one in the hotel had seen Mrs. Stanfield that day.

She had not phoned for breakfast.

Maria Elena Garcia, who had charge of this floor and who personally cleaned the suite, had respected the sign on the door. No, it had never been hung out before by Mrs. Stanfield.

From Biersma on down, no one expressed any concern about Pauline Stanfield. They were all anxious to escape any criticism or responsibility. It seemed clear to Gerald that the cleaning lady did not care for Pauline.

When Cleary showed up, he had a toothpick in his mouth and Gerald realized he was hungry. He suggested they adjourn to the Eye in the Sky and have lunch there.

"It doesn't open until three," Biersma said.

"I'll call room service," Gerald said. "Andrew, what would you like?"

He looked at Gerald as if he had forgotten what food is. "Anything. I don't care."

Gerald had them send up turkey sandwiches and milk. His anxiety about Pauline decreased as Andrew's increased. Cleary had one of his deputies stop by the Stanfield house, and Pauline wasn't there.

"She must still be in the hotel," Gerald said.

Andrew turned. "Why do you say that?"

"She was here yesterday. No one saw her today. So she must still be here."

"That's why she's not in her room?"

The sandwiches arrived and Gerald did not reply. There was nothing wrong with his logic. And when the bartender of the Eye in the Sky came in at three, his surmise looked even more solid. His name was Bruce and his face was almost as white as his shirt. He drew on his filtered cigarette and then nodded as he exhaled.

"She was in the lounge last night. For maybe an hour. She met a guy and they left." His eyes darted from Andrew to Biersma. "Another guest."

"What is his name?"

The corners of Bruce's mouth went down as his brows went up. He didn't know. Could he describe him? He could, in some detail, but the description meant nothing to anyone until Biersma called down for the registration list for yesterday. It took ten minutes before it was clear that Bruce had described Bernard Lynch from Minneapolis.

"Professor Bernard Lynch," Biersma noted.

"What room?"

Perhaps if they had learned of Lynch earlier, it would have seemed a delicate matter to knock on his door to see if Pauline Stanfield was with him, but as it was they all took the elevator down two floors and marched to Lynch's door. Biersma knocked authoritatively and then frowned at the ceiling. In five seconds he knocked again. Already he was fingering a key.

"Open it up," Andrew said.

"Sheriff?"

Cleary, pleased to be consulted, nodded. "Open the door."

And then they were all in another empty room. The bathroom had not been used, the bed had not been slept in. Biersma held up his hand.

"This room was cleaned this morning."

"Find out if Lynch checked out."

But there was no need for that. He had paid for the room when he registered. Paid in cash. Presumably, he had spent the night and left that morning. Whether he had spent the night with Pauline Stanfield was anyone's guess.

"I'm more interested to know if she is spending the day with him."

What a hell of a day. Gerald had gone on a simple and by then familiar errand, to fetch Pauline Stanfield from the Ben Hur, and then had spent most of the day in the hotel with ambiguous results. He summed it up for Andrew.

Pauline was not in the Ben Hur. At least, she was not in her suite and not in Lynch's room. She had a couple of drinks with the professor in the Eye in the Sky last night. Bruce said they had left together, but from the time they left the lounge, Pauline had been seen by no one.

Andrew said, "It looks as if they went to her room, not his."

"The bed?"

Andrew nodded. "It looks a lot more like a fight than lovemaking to me, Gerald. Why was the phone ripped out of the wall? Why was the clothesline pulled out of the wall?''

"The phone might just have been disconnected?''

"The Garcia woman said the furniture in the sitting room was out of place.''

"What are you suggesting?''

"I don't know. But I want to meet Professor Bernard Lynch.''

"So do I. Did you see what he put on the registration card?''

"What's that?''

"He said he was driving an Edsel.''

TWENTY-NINE

WHEN NOREEN pulled into the parking lot of the country club, she saw that Leo's car was already there, and he was sitting in it. His hand lifted in greeting and he rolled down the window as she came toward him.

"I wanted to catch the end of the news before going in."

"Go ahead."

He pushed open the door, leaving the radio on. It was just the local news. In a moment he turned it off and got out of the car. They were almost equal in height and she wasn't wearing heels, but it didn't bother her any. She preferred flats. Just walking across the parking lot to the club seemed significant, although Noreen did not know exactly what Leo's attitude toward her was.

When talking of his parents had made him break down, she felt a great tenderness toward him. Love? She wasn't sure what love was. Once she had thought she loved Harry, but if that was love, she wanted no more of it. As for what she'd had with Hal Stanfield, well, she didn't even want to think of that. She had been cheapened by that relationship and dreaded having to talk about it with Leo. But somehow she knew that until they talked about it, nothing could happen between them.

Daydreaming of being married to Leo Barany had become her favorite indoor sport, and the more she thought of it, the more she liked it. What if they were to marry and she no longer had to work! Oh, she wouldn't mind a little part-time work, just to bring in extra money, if they needed it, but not to have to face it every day. She could do a lot worse than wait on tables, she knew that. The hours were bad but there weren't that many of them, and at the club there was a sure 15 percent tip from every table, and the fringes were good, an excellent medical plan. She certainly didn't want to lose that. The truth was, she had no idea what marriage would mean, but it was a pleasant thought that he liked her, that they got along, that she had seen him cry. That bound them together more than anything.

"What happened to your face, Leo?"

His hand went to the scratch on his cheek. "I cut myself shaving."

"You should get an electric razor."

"Good idea."

"Let me see." But before she could touch his face, he twisted away.

"It's all right! I put something on it."

Noreen stopped and so did he. "You don't like people touching you, do you?"

"Why do you say that?"

"It's true, isn't it?"

She had the sense that this would be the end of them or a real beginning. What she had said might sound like an attack on his manhood and she knew what that could do to the male ego, but that isn't how she meant it.

"People?"

She smiled and he did too, and she put her arm through his and they went on into the club.

Her tables filled early and were never empty throughout the lunch period, but being busy did not stop her mind from being pleasantly abuzz. When she hurried into the bar for drinks, she and Leo seemed to communicate without saying a thing. There was really nothing different at all, yet everything had changed and the other girls noticed. But Noreen just ignored the knowing looks and discouraged all questions, and when the last diners had signed their checks and gone, she slid onto a stool. Leo put a glass of chablis before her.

"Aren't you having any?"

"Bartenders never drink."

"Well, waitresses wait."

"I'll be right with you."

They took her car and went to her place and right into the bedroom where, without a word, methodically, he made love to her. It was good. It was just fine. It was the best of Harry and Hal Stanfield with none of the negatives. Afterward, he lay his head on her breast and she pressed him close.

"We're touching."

"I noticed."

"You want coffee, I'll make some."

He shook his head and got out of bed. "I'll make it."

He didn't put anything on before going into the kitchen. Smiling, Noreen pulled the sheet to her chin and looked at the ceiling. In the kitchen the radio went on and he turned the dial. But it was the news he wanted, not music. He didn't come back until it was over.

"What's new?"

"Nothing." He stood beside the bed and she had to look him in the eye. She put out her hand and tugged him back to her. He fell asleep. On one elbow she studied him as he slept. The cut on his face looked more like a scratch than anything. Noreen couldn't care less how he had got it. That cut had finally broken the ice between them.

When she took a shower, she did not lock the bathroom door, but he didn't come in. He was lying in bed awake when she came out, toweling her hair.

"It's all yours."

He nodded. "In a minute."

"You could sleep a little more if you want."

He wanted. She had to shake him awake so they wouldn't be late getting back to the club. Well, it took a lot more out of a man.

On the drive back he turned on the car radio and that is when they learned that Pauline Stanfield was missing. She waited for him to say something, but he didn't, so she said, "If everyone not seen for a few hours was declared missing, who wouldn't be?"

"If you don't step on it, we'll be."

"I told you she wouldn't be accused of her husband's death."

"Maybe she didn't kill him."

"And maybe she did."

"Then she'll pay for it."

"When, in the next world?"

He stared straight ahead, not quite smiling.

THIRTY

ANDREW SENT GERALD to Minneapolis to interview Professor Bernard Lynch once he had made certain that such a person existed. Lynch was an associate professor of English at the University of Minnesota, but Gerald tracked him down at St. Mary's Hospital in Rochester where he was recovering from a gallstone operation. The operation had been performed on August 24, making it unlikely that he had been in Wyler, Indiana, romancing Pauline Stanfield in the Eye in the Sky that same night. But he could have been staying in the Ben Hur for all that it would have mattered. Professor Lynch was short and bald and overweight, not at all like his impersonator.

"What was his reaction when you told him?"

Gerald shrugged. "He asked me if I had read Graham Greene's autobiography."

"The writer?"

"He's one of Lynch's specialties. Apparently, Greene was plagued for years by someone impersonating him around the world."

"Did he have any guesses as to who the man in the Ben Hur might be?"

"He couldn't imagine why anyone would want to imitate him anywhere, let alone in Indiana. The best he could come up with was that it might have been a former student."

"How long has he been teaching?"

"I had the same thought. There could be thousands of them."

Gerald had not let it go at that, but questioned Lynch to see if he had any knowledge of or connection with the Stanfields or Wyler or the Ben Hur. Nothing.

Cleary declared Pauline missing and sent out information on her, but it seemed roughly equivalent to buying a ticket in the lottery. Losing two clients, one to a still undiscovered murderer, the other to a Lothario posing as a professor, made Andrew difficult to live with, and when Susannah began to blame herself for not insisting that Pauline accept her invitation to dinner on the twenty-fourth, he blew up at her.

"For God's sake, Susannah. Pauline is an adult. You're not responsible for her. I'm not responsible for her. If she wants to pick up a stranger in a bar right after Hal has been brutally killed, well, that's her privilege. She is going to surface in Florida or Jamaica or some other place and wonder what all the fuss was about. I am through worrying about her."

Susannah said nothing, just hugged his arm. She should have hit him. He told her so and she shook her head.

"Look what happened to Hal."

The mild attempt at humor set Andrew's mind going. Imagine that what had happened to Hal was meant as punishment for striking Pauline in public. A secret admirer? Who then sought Pauline out in the bar at the Ben Hur and ran away with her? Maybe he should have Cleary get in a police artist and try to construct a picture from the descriptions of the phony Professor Lynch the bartender of the Eye in the Sky and the girl at the registration desk had given. The only problem with that was that the descriptions did not sound as if they were of the same man.

He kissed Susannah on the cheek, apologized for snapping at her, and when she had left the office, put through a call to Silvia Wood. No wife in the world could be expected to ignore her husband's wanting a confidential conversation with Silvia Wood. He made an appointment for a haircut.

"I'll cut it myself," Silvia said.

Andrew Broom did not approve of unisex shops—combination barber shops and beauty parlors—but if he had to be in one, he preferred having an honest-to-God woman like Silvia cutting his hair rather than one of those limp-wristed hair stylists who never seemed to lose sight of themselves in the mirror. Andrew was able to keep his eye on Silvia in the mirror as they talked.

"Any idea where she went, Silvia?"

Her perfume was just one more scent here, but it did not lose its power to corrode the moral fiber of the male who came within its range. Andrew was glad Susannah could not see this beautiful young woman hovering over him. Surely, there is something intrinsically erotic about a woman's cutting a man's hair. Had Freud written of a Samson complex?

"She was a dreamer. She talked a lot about going off to exotic places, picking up guys, the whole bit. But she wouldn't have gone to Chicago without getting permission from Hal."

"It was in Chicago that she ran around with a man named Corbett. Was there anyone else?"

"Not that I know of."

"She confided in you, didn't she?"

"Yes."

"So did Hal?"

"He told me to tell no one he was a partner in these parlors. Particularly not to tell you."

"Why?"

"I don't know. Maybe he was a little ashamed of it. Would you have invested in this place?"

"You're cutting my hair, aren't you? How much is this going to cost me?"

"You can afford it."

"Let me tell you of my theory."

The trick was to connect Hal's death and Pauline's disappearance, and since Silvia had known the Stanfields in an unusual way, that should pose no problem for her. Some gallant soul, appalled at Hal's treatment of his wife, kills him and then seeks her out.

"Some member of the country club?"

"Any ideas?"

"You."

"Ha."

"She had a crush on you, Andrew. Pauline. Surely, you must have noticed."

That was as good a reason as any to drop his theory. "Tell me this, Silvia—when Pauline came to your place, I mean on the night of August sixteenth, did she tell you she came from home?"

"She said she had been driving around."

"There's no doubt she was in the house that night." He told her about the bourbon, the turned-down bed, the fact that the shower had been used.

"I thought you were trying to prove she didn't kill Hal."

"What's your gut opinion on that, Silvia?"

Silvia had stepped back to examine her handiwork. Their eyes met in the mirror. "She could have done it, if she was mad enough. I'm surprised she didn't try to kill him at the time he hit her."

"She was at a bit of a disadvantage lying on the floor."

Imagine that Pauline was guilty, that she had toughed it out until there was no chance charges would be brought against her, and then, relieved but still scared, she just took off. Maybe the phony professor had been in on it and now that the coast was clear they cleared out.

The trouble with theories was that there were dozens of them which, however implausible, were logically possible. Logical possibility meant nothing at all. Neither did plausibility. The only thing that mattered finally were facts, and Andrew Broom had never before felt that he knew so little of something he was supposedly involved in.

Hal had been his client. He had been, in some broad sense of the word, his friend. Andrew had known Hal and Pauline for years. During the past week he had talked with Pauline once a day and yet her disappearance came as a total surprise. He could not believe that she had just disappeared. The reason he got angry with Susannah for trying to take the blame for what had happened to the Stanfields was that, in a way, he blamed himself. He had stopped resisting their constant threats of divorce and had told her to go ahead if that was what she wanted to do. What either one imagined doing without the other mystified him. They made asses out of themselves pretty well with one another, so they didn't need freedom for that. It came down to this—that he had not taken Hal and Pauline seriously. And now Hal was dead and Pauline was missing.

Missing. What the hell did that mean, other than that someone's whereabouts were unknown to someone else?

"The point is that the ones who don't know should know. That's why they report it." Cleary took obvious pleasure in instructing Andrew Broom.

"How many people are reported missing in this county in a year?"

"What difference does it make how many?" Cleary easily took offense. Did he think it was a criticism of his county that he couldn't claim a large number of missing persons?

"How many?"

"This year? Two. Counting Mrs. Stanfield."

"Who's the other?"

"A man named Slattery."

THIRTY-ONE

WITH THE STANFIELD WOMAN it had been getting even, a punishment, closer to rape than romance except that she had loved it, but with Noreen . . . Leo Barany was at a loss for words.

Not only was she beautiful, not only was she self-reliant, supporting herself and her child without complaint, taking abuse from club members like Pauline Stanfield, but she liked him. He had never been so comfortable with anyone before, man or woman. Going to bed with her was not something he wanted to drive from his mind afterward, something dirty, only to be forgotten. He wanted to recall every moment of being with her as if it had been a holy time.

That thought would have brought derisive laughter from the Leo Barany of only a few days ago, but Noreen had given him back his childhood innocence. He couldn't explain it and it didn't bother him that he couldn't. But this return of childlike wonder was a mixed blessing. Suddenly, he saw what he had done to his parents and Slattery and Hal Stanfield, and just last night to Pauline Stanfield, with Noreen's eyes, and he was disgusted and horrified.

Getting Pauline down to the basement garage in the garment bag had been a chore until he decided to drag rather than carry the body, but even so it was not easy. The chances of running into anyone in that stairway were nil, he kept telling himself—maybe he even believed it—but until he got to the garage, anything might happen.

It didn't happen until he got to the garage. He had picked up the garment bag in both arms and pushed the door into the garage open with his shoulder, and suddenly he was staring a man right in the eyes. The man stepped back, holding the door, and executed a bow that nearly cost him his balance.

"*Après vous, monsieur,*" he said. He was very drunk.

"*Merci beaucoup.*"

"*De nada.*"

Barany wondered where the guy had been until after 3 A.M. in Wyler, but he went on past him, trying not to stagger under the weight of Pauline's body. When he got to his car, he turned. The stairway door had closed before the drunk got through it, and now he was struggling with it, trying to get it open. At this hour the door was locked and could only be opened with a hotel key. Why didn't the guy take the elevator? Barany didn't like having even a drunk around when he opened the trunk of his car and dumped in the garment bag containing the body of Pauline Stanfield, but he had no choice. Besides, he had a lot to do before he slept.

The drunk induced caution and Leo drove to Privett well within the speed limit. He himself had drunk more tonight than he had in years and he did not want to attract any police notice. Once he got on the Wabash Road, he didn't see any kind of car, and he could imagine he was alone in the world, the last survivor, all his enemies dead. The night was bright, the new moon only a few days old. He could have driven without lights. He tried it, dousing the headlights, and after a moment it was no trouble at all. But he switched them on again. It was the sort of dumb thing that could lead to trouble and he had all the trouble he needed in the trunk.

By the time he pulled into his driveway, his anxiety had increased. He wouldn't be able to relax until he got rid of that body. When he left Wyler, he thought he might just dump the garment bag into the metal shed for the night and bury it in the morning, but now that seemed fraught with risk. He lugged Pauline right out to the shed and got to work digging.

He started on the far side of the shed, right next to the wall, figuring he would go four or five feet and then dig sideways so that the body would be under the concrete floor of the shed with the others. But when he had a good deep hole, he climbed out and tumbled the body in and began to fill it up again almost frantically. When he was done, he stood panting in the moonlight and looked off toward the horizon. Nothing in that direction but the Walnut Grove Golf Course. He'd smoothed up around the new grave, but he knew that a lot more would have to be done in daylight.

It was going on five when he went inside, where he showered away the clay and mud but could not rid his mind of thoughts of the shower in the Ben Hur Hotel. He turned off the shower and let the tub fill and sat in hot water to his armpits until he fell asleep.

When he awoke, the water was lapping at his chin because he had slid down. If he were shorter he might have slipped under entirely. Was it possible to drown in one's sleep? Leo thought it would wake you up. But if it didn't, that wouldn't be a bad way to go, enveloped by water like a baby in the womb, swimming toward death this time, not birth.

He worked the plug free with his foot and turned on the hot water, raising the temperature. When it was as hot as he could bear, he turned off the water and replaced the plug. It was eight o'clock. By the time he thought of listening to the news, it was too late, so he settled back again and relaxed. Five people had gone to their deaths because of him. It didn't seem so bad. Maybe he had done them a favor; in his mother's case he was almost sure he had. What difference did a few years make one way or the other? Leo told himself that if he had slipped beneath the water of the tub and drowned it would have been okay with him. To die, to sleep... His conscience made no coward of him. Leo Barany believed that when you died it was all over. Dreams of immortality were pathetic, a refusal to accept the fact that there is no more chance of our living after we die than there was of our having lived before we were conceived.

By the time he got out of the tub and dried off and went into the kitchen to put water on for tea, Leo had adjusted to the fact that he had removed Pauline Stanfield from the land of the living. She had deserved to die. He had only been an instrument. An instrument of what? No need to probe the metaphor; he knew what he meant.

On the way to work he had the radio on, just in case there was some bulletin about Pauline Stanfield, but he really didn't expect any. He didn't expect it on the regular news either, but he waited for it to come on after he had parked at the club. Noreen came over to talk and they went into the club together.

It was her challenging him before they went inside that marked the change between them. Was he really afraid of being touched? Not by her. When she put it to him and they stood looking at one another, he remembered, as he was certain she did, how he had broken down that day at the house when he felt her hand lie gently on his shoulder.

Throughout the period when lunch was served and she was darting in and out of the bar and he was busy making drinks for her and the other waitresses, Leo felt that something was going to happen, something good. He felt wonderful, as if he had had a good night's sleep. Noreen felt the same way he did, he could sense it, and apparently others could as well.

When the break came, they went to her apartment and just walked on into the bedroom and without a word undressed and got into her bed. It was their wedding ceremony. They belonged to one another now. It had been holy.

Back behind his bar, glad to be busy, Leo went over the events of the past weeks, looking for anything that might jeopardize what he now had with Noreen. If this had happened earlier, five people might still be alive. Leo really believed that. He would have spared them all if he'd had Noreen. Telesales, bartending—he would have done anything to support them. Who needed money, really? The simple life. In bed with a woman you loved. What else was there, really?

So it was more important than ever that no one could connect him with the death of Hal Stanfield or with what they were calling the disappearance of Pauline. Leo tried to reconstruct the scene at the Eye in the Sky. Had anyone really noticed him? The bartender would have. Leo knew that bartenders saw everything. And there had been people at the desk when he checked in. Now he knew that he could have taken care of Pauline without going through the bother of renting a room himself. All he would have had to do was show up at the Eye in the Sky, sit down next to Pauline, and everything would have unfolded as it had. But he had no way of knowing that before the fact. So at least the bartender and the girl who checked him into the hotel had seen him. They must have been questioned by the sheriff and they would have described the man with whom Pauline was last seen.

Leo thought of the worst case. Say he was identified as the man who'd had a few drinks with Pauline Stanfield in the bar on top of the First Bank Building last night. So what? He had just gone there for a drink, had recognized Mrs. Stanfield from the club. Wasn't he the guy who had tried to stop her husband from hitting her? So they had a few drinks together and afterward she went to her room, presumably, and he drove home to Privett. Sure. a perfectly plausible story, if he ever had to use it. Nonetheless, Leo Barany felt uneasy. Anything that endangered what he had with Noreen was bound to make him uneasy. The sooner they got away from Wyler the better.

The problem with that was that he couldn't sell the house or inherit anything for years.

He assured himself that he was in no danger.

That night, after their dinner stint was done, Noreen wanted to go back to the house in Privett with him.

"My mother's watching Karen. I already arranged it."

"I won't be much company. I'm really beat."

She smiled and took his hand. "It's not just your body I'm after, Leo."

She wanted to walk around the property, but he steered her wide of the shed and onto the Walnut Grove Golf Course, where even in the twilight people were still golfing. They sat on a bench above the fourteenth tee, and in the distance they could see the taller buildings in Wyler: the Hoosier Towers; the First Bank Building.

"Have you ever been in the lounge on the top floor?" Noreen asked.

"The Eye in the Sky? Yeah, I checked it out."

"I've never been there."

Leo felt awful, as if he were establishing an alibi with Noreen. God, if only he could tell her everything, but all he had to do was imagine her reaction. Sweetie, I've killed five people recently, four of them are buried in the backyard, but I'm turning over a new leaf, now that we've gotten together. How she would loathe him if she knew. He loathed himself now when he thought of what he had done.

But all his fears were imaginary—what might happen if something else happened, the consequences if this or that were done—and after a week Leo settled down. The past was the past and he intended to live in the present with Noreen.

And then he got the call from Silvia Wood.

THIRTY-TWO

THE FIRST THING you learned about people and their resolutions is that they don't keep them. It doesn't matter that their health and looks are involved, most people will keep on a schedule for a while and then, sooner rather than later, they taper off and quit. Silvia had a variety of plans designed to counter this natural tendency, contracts that locked the client in for months, but even when they had in effect already paid for tanning sessions, people would stop coming.

Telephone reminders—no nagging, just reminders that depended on the client's conscience to do the nagging—a series of postcards, wittily done, beautifully designed, sent First Class mail, helped. Silvia made the phone calls herself just as she was the one who sat down with the client when a contract was signed. Her good name was at stake and she wanted customers to know it.

After cutting Andrew Broom's hair, Silvia went into her office, locked the door, turned on the vent, and lit a joint. The conversation with Broom had reminded her how vulnerable she was. Her roots were not in Wyler, and no matter how well she had done here, no matter that several dozen people were gainfully employed who might not be if it weren't for her enterprise in starting these parlors, Silvia knew that if any cloud were cast over her or her operation, she could be put out of business in short order. And at the moment she couldn't think of anyone who would really mourn if it happened. Hence the smoke.

Broom thought she knew more than she did, probably because she hadn't told Gerald the first time they talked that Hal had stopped by her place on the night of the sixteenth. Stopped by. Andrew Broom knew Hal better than she did and he was unlikely to think Hal had come up for a cup of tea. The coroner's report indicated that Hal had been smoking marijuana hours before he died. It would take an idiot not to wonder if he had been with her when he smoked the pot, and Andrew Broom was no idiot. So why hadn't he asked? If he had, she would have told him Hal smoked the pot at her place. Not that she would reveal that it was hers and she who offered it to him. But having that known was a hell of a lot better than having it suspected and unmentioned.

It was dumb to smoke in her office, but sometimes being dumb was a necessity. She took a deep drag, closed her eyes, and swallowed it. That quick her head felt big as the Goodyear blimp, which is what she had been after. She pinched the joint and put it back in the lozenge tin, which she returned to the very back of the central drawer of her desk.

But she couldn't stay high forever, and in the subsequent days her anxiety increased. She had to distract herself with something constructive. That is when she got out the list of delinquent clients and her eye fell on the name of Leo Barany. The bartender at the country club, a good-looking man but shy. It had been a month since he came for a session. Not that he had signed a contract. Silvia had spent an hour trying in vain to get him to sign up. He said he didn't need a contract. Well, she would use a mild version of "I told you so" and try to get him back. Bartenders did not have time to lie in the sun and get a natural tan. Not that the sun was a legitimate competitor. Silvia did not disguise the dangers of exposing the flesh to the sun. Fear of cancer was her greatest ally.

But Leo Barany's name brought back the unsettling conversation with Andrew Broom, and she picked up the phone and dialed the number typed on the card. As bartender at the country club Barany might well know if Broom's guess had any substance. Had Pauline been seeing some guy?

"I don't have time," he said when she got through to him at the club.

"When can I call back?"

"I mean I don't have time for tanning sessions. I thought I would, but I don't."

"Leo, we wouldn't have time for meals if we didn't make time."

"Maybe next month."

"Good. In the meantime, I'd like to talk with you." She couldn't wait until next month, and if getting through to him as a client didn't work, she would try the direct approach.

"Go ahead."

"In person. Could you come here?"

"Talk about what?"

"Do you know the lawyer Andrew Broom?"

"He's a member here."

"He has asked me some questions and I think you can help me with the answers."

There was a long silence during which Silvia's lips moved in prayer. St. Francis would not let her down, she was sure of it. He didn't. Leo said he would drop by that afternoon, before three.

She saw him drive in, but he remained in his car. Silvia tapped on the window, but he indicated she should come out. What could she do? When she opened the door and stepped into the late August afternoon from the air-conditioned interior of her salon, she paused, then ran to the car and pulled open the door and slipped in.

"How's business in weather like this?"

"Come on inside."

"I'm inside all day. I thought we could drive and talk. Okay?"

"I better tell them I'm going."

"We won't be gone that long." And he started off. At least the car was air-conditioned. "Light us up. They're in the glove compartment."

"Cigarettes?"

He grinned without turning toward her. Silvia might have played dumb, but she was curious. There was a plastic bag in the glove compartment with several joints among the loose marijuana. She decided against pretending shock, extracted one of the joints, lit it, and passed it to Leo. He glanced at her briefly as he took it. Silvia decided that she liked him. She needed to feel close to someone, and what had happened to Hal and Pauline made her feel abandoned. He handed her the joint and she took a deep drag.

"Good stuff. Where do you get it?"

"I grow it."

"You're kidding."

"I have a very versatile garden."

"Where?"

"I'll show you."

"You said we wouldn't be gone long."

"Think of it as customer relations."

She laughed. She had never thought of him as fun before, but this was a new Leo Barany, not the shy man who'd asked about a tanning session as if he were about to lose his virginity. "Tell me how you knew I'd light up."

"I studied psychology."

"Aren't you the smart one."

He said something and she didn't understand a word.

"What was that?"

"Old English."

"That's a furniture polish."

His laughter seemed to come from the pit of his stomach, but it was a conspiratorial laughter and Silvia felt even better. The plastic bag, Leo's friendliness, a ride in the country—she hadn't felt this good in weeks.

"Where is your garden?"

"We're nearly there."

They were nearly to Privett when he pulled off the road and up a long driveway.

"Whose house?"

"Mine." The list she had been working from that morning came back to her. This was the address he had given when he came to the salon.

"We'll get out of the heat in a minute, but first come see my garden."

He took her hand and they swung around the house and started across the lawn toward a metal shed.

"I want to pick up a shovel," he explained as he unlocked the door, pulled it open, and stepped back.

He gestured, indicating she could inspect the interior. Silvia shrugged. When in the country... She stooped and put her head inside the little door. It was very dark, and hot as an oven.

She felt the blow on the back of her neck, but before she fell forward into oblivion, he struck her again.

THIRTY-THREE

HE TOLD NEITHER SUSANNAH nor Gerald what he was doing, maybe because he wasn't so sure what it was himself. The only reason he was asking about the disappearance of James Slattery was that he was one of two missing persons in the county this year. Pauline being the other, if she was missing. If a lost person knows where he is, is he lost? He had the feeling that somewhere Pauline was just raising hell and here he was trying to figure out where she had gone and the best he could think to do was ask about James Slattery.

That Slattery had been missing since early summer was clear enough. He was a widower with a daughter living in Oregon, but he had not gone to see her. The high school where he taught employed him in driver training during the summer, and he was as reliable a person as one could wish, patient with the kids, a great baseball fan, the Cardinals being his team. One day he had finished his work at the school, told one or two people he would see them the following day, and disappeared from the face of the earth. Cleary let Andrew into Slattery's house, and he wandered through the rooms, breathing the dead hot air, trying to imagine the life that had been lived there. The chair in front of the television was the most comfortable one in the house. Under his mattress Slattery had hidden some girlie magazines, but a rosary dangled from the bedpost. There was a wall phone in the kitchen and beside it a board on which numbers were scribbled.

"Did you try all these?"

"I think so," Cleary said.

Andrew copied them down. Five in all. The sixth was a long-distance number, the daughter in Oregon. Husbands desert their families and are never found, but they are not thought of as missing. Children are another thing. God knows what happens to them. But this county could boast a missing widower and a widow, neither of whom was fleeing anything. If they had wanted to travel, they could have traveled, said good-bye and been off with no mystery at all. But that is not what had happened. The county had never before had one case like this, let alone two.

Andrew had Cleary call the sheriff in Privett to pave the way for his visit. Expanding his inquiries did not make them seem less pointless, but he would rather be doing something stupid than nothing at all.

Sheriff Erlanger was cooperative enough, though he seemed a little wary. What had Cleary told him? He gave Andrew a list with seven names on it. His county's missing persons.

"All of them this year?"

"That's right."

"How many ever turn up, on the average?"

"Maybe one or two of them will. Last year a fellow in a plane spotted a car in the river, and when we fished it out, it was a middle-aged woman who had been reported missing. Her family had no explanation and it was a great mystery. What happened is she had a heart attack and her car went into the river and there she had been all along."

Andrew looked at the list he held. It was a printout so light he could scarcely read it. What was he supposed to do, hold it over a flame? He took it to the window. The third and fourth names rang a bell.

"Barany," he said aloud.

"Mister and Missus," Erlanger said. "Lived out on the Wabash Road. Reported missing last May."

"By whom?"

"The son."

"What's his name?"

"Leo."

Leo Barany. The bartender at the country club? He asked Erlanger to tell him about Leo Barany, and it didn't sound much like the man who worked behind the bar at the country club. Graduate of Purdue, gone on to do graduate work.

"Where?"

Erlanger looked up from the report he had been reading. "The way he reported his folks missing, he phoned here and said they hadn't answered their phone for days and would someone check the house."

"Where was he calling from?"

"That I do have. Minneapolis."

Andrew Broom got the address of the house on the Wabash Road. He could go by the place on his way back to Wyler.

THIRTY-FOUR

NOREEN FRESHENED UP and came into the lounge expecting to find Leo, but Harrison was behind the bar, fussing none too happily through the records of the drinks ordered during the lunch period.

"Where's Leo?"

"On the phone in my office." Harrison obviously did not like it. "Someone called and just had to speak with him."

"I wonder who," Noreen said casually.

"I don't care who she is, my phone is not public. What I want to know is whether Leo gave her my number. I'll be damned if I'll run errands for my bartenders."

Noreen went into the dining room and stood by a window looking out at the golfers waiting to tee off. What an idiot game golf was. Maybe all games are idiotic. From time to time, she turned and looked toward the bar to see if Leo had come back. But it was nearly five minutes more before he appeared. She hurried toward him, smiling; these next few hours were their special time.

"I've got to run an errand," he said when Harrison was gone.

"That's all right."

He shook his head. "No, I don't want to ruin your break. Look, go to your place and I'll try to get there before it's time to come back."

He was lying. She knew it. She had been lied to by experts and amateurs and all kinds, but the kind of liar Leo reminded her of was Hal Stanfield.

"If you can make it."

He took her hand and squeezed it. There are so many ways to lie. Noreen felt that they were separated by something like Saran Wrap; it was there and you couldn't see it but it had two sides, his and hers, and the single thing they had been for a few days was now divided. If he had told her he wanted to spend the next few hours with another woman it would have been easier than this. The truth is always better than lies. She was certain she really believed that.

She went on ahead, out to her car, which gave her the usual trouble but finally started. After leaving the lot, when she was hidden by the hedge that lined the drive, Noreen turned to the left and went up the looping road that brought cars back through the great porte-cochere of the club. She was already turned around when Leo's car went past on the lower drive. Noreen continued on down and followed him in the direction of Wyler.

If she didn't think about what she was doing, it was better, because all she had to do was imagine some other woman doing what she was doing and she knew what she would think. Leo wasn't her husband, they hadn't even talked marriage, they had spent a few hours together and, yes, they had gone to bed, but who in the world imagined that meant anything? Noreen did, that's who. Not even with Hal Stanfield could she think of it as what it was, an afternoon in a motel with no future to it. He was using her and she had let him and it was awful. She did not want to remember that she had followed Hal like this because with Leo it was different. He didn't have a wife. She was certain he was not the same kind of man Hal Stanfield had been. If he was lying to her, it was because he loved her.

Once she hit on that explanation, it was a lot easier to follow Leo into Wyler, to keep back out of sight so he wouldn't see her. Why should he think he was being followed? Did she think she was? She looked in the rearview mirror, but a glance told nothing.

When he pulled up in front of the tanning salon, Noreen drove on past to a McDonald's, where she cut through and back around, then parked across the street from the salon. Leo was still in his car, waiting, and then the woman came out and jumped in. Noreen had only a glimpse, but it was enough to make her heart sink. She was beautiful. Glamorous. Sexy. Above all, sexy. And Noreen was sure she had seen her somewhere before. My God, of course, it was Silvia Wood! She felt she was reliving the awful times with Hal.

Leo was pulling out into the street, and Noreen leaned over on the seat, waited until she was sure he was past, then made a U-turn that enraged half a dozen drivers who pressed on their horns and shook their heads, but she didn't care. She had to keep following Leo now.

In ten minutes she realized he was heading home with Silvia, and the way they were talking removed her last hope. Silvia must be years older than Leo; there had to be some perfectly innocent explanation. But Silvia and Leo were sharing a cigarette. Silvia sat sideways in her seat, jabbering away to him, from time to time offering him the cigarette. There was no way Noreen could avoid thinking that they intended to spend these afternoon hours the same way she and Leo had spent them only yesterday.

She hated him. He was no different from Harry or from Hal Stanfield. At the moment, Leo Barany was every man who had ever betrayed any woman, a malevolent force. Her foot itched to stamp down on the gas.

She would have liked to floor it and drive into the back
of his car at full speed and just keep pushing him down
the road, as fast as she could, until... Until they were all
killed? She shook her head. She did not want to die.
Certainly not for Leo Barany. To hell with him. To hell
with all men. He *deserved* someone like Silvia Wood. No.
It was Silvia she should feel solidarity with. What did a
woman of her accomplishments want with a creep like
Leo Barany?

Noreen was no more than twenty-five yards behind Leo
when he turned into his driveway. She continued on out
of sight and pulled to the side of the road along a fairway of the Walnut Grove Golf Course.

Having turned off the engine and rolled down a window, Noreen was assailed by the country sounds of late
summer. Weedlike flowers beside the road were host to
bees; on the hot afternoon air the songs of birds seemed
to distribute notes along the staff of wires that stretched
from pole to pole. But it was the steady buzz of insects,
the hum of life, one generation preparing for the next, the
natural cycle being repeated to infinity. And here she was,
parked on the side of the road in the middle of an August afternoon, making a fool of herself.

She got out of the car, easing the door shut as if she
feared disturbing the natural life teeming around her.
Walking up the road to the house was out of the question, but then simply being here was out of the question.
She went around the car and through a shallow ditch and
came up into the weedy fringe that ran along the golf
course fence. Running her fingers along the diamond
shapes formed by the wire of the fence, Noreen walked
in the direction of the Barany house. The fence reached
a corner and she turned it and came to a fragrant pile of
cut grass. Opposite it was a gate in the fence. Unlocked.

Noreen went through and walked to where she was certain she could see the house.

She stopped and leaned against a tree for support when she saw Leo crossing the lawn with Silvia. They looked like the last couple on earth. Or the first. Noreen had the dreadful certainty that her worst fears were going to be realized right before her eyes.

Leo had stopped at the shed in the backyard and then unlocked the door. It was like a silent movie, the way he stepped back and bowed low. In the shed? Noreen couldn't believe it. But Leo had picked up something from behind the shed, a shovel.

It happened so fast, Noreen hardly believed her eyes. Leo pushed Silvia and at the same time brought a shovel down on the back of her head. Then he struck her again, threw down the shovel, and was pushing the fallen Silvia into the shed. He slammed the door, locked it, and then looked quickly around.

She drew back behind the tree. Her fingers were digging into the bark and she was aware of the resinous smell of pine. She pressed her cheek against the tree and moved her head slightly. Leo was strolling back across the lawn to the house. Alone. If he left Silvia in that hot shed, she could . . .

Die? Of course. That is what he intended to happen.

Noreen pushed away from the tree and moved to a bench, where she sat down as if she had been dropped. Next to the bench was a ball washer, a faint smell of soap, a towel hanging in limp surrender. It might have been her emblem. She could not stop the thoughts that marched through her mind, one growing out of the other, the whole making sense, forming an argument. An indictment. Noreen knew things she did not know she knew. Things about Leo. Leo and the Stanfields.

For example, the attention he paid to the news broadcasts. What was he expecting to hear? Things he already knew and wondered when others would. Like the disappearance of Pauline Stanfield. Noreen thought of the scratch on Leo's face and his reaction when she tried to touch it. Then everything had changed between them. Why? Did he make love to her so she wouldn't wonder how he had gotten scratched?

She stood up. Her impulse was to go through the trees and onto the Barany lawn and get Silvia out of that metal shed. The sun beat down relentlessly. She would be baked to death in there. But Leo had locked the door. She could not open a locked door with her bare hands. She had to go for help.

She retraced her steps, to the open gate, past the mound of mown grass, sweetly rotten in the sun, and along the fence to the car. As she got into the car, she looked up the road, fearful that she would see Leo. But there was no sign of him. She settled with a sigh behind the wheel. Now if only the engine would start.

There was a sound in the seat behind her and Noreen, about to insert the ignition key, froze. Her eyes lifted to the rearview mirror.

Leo Barany stared back at her.

"So you came to me," he said.

THIRTY-FIVE

ANDREW BROOM had driven along the Wabash Road whenever he golfed at Walnut Grove, but this was the first time he really noticed the houses on either side of the road. Checking the numbers on the mailboxes, hoping the name as well as the number would be on the Baranys', he arrived at the driveway at the same time as a car coming in the opposite direction. He slowed; so did the Olds. Andrew flicked his directional signal, indicating he meant to take a left turn, but the car entered the Barany driveway before him. The woman at the wheel looked at him strangely and her face seemed familiar. Then Andrew noticed the man in the back seat. Odd.

Andrew followed the car up the driveway. There was another car already parked in front of the closed garage doors.

The back door of the Olds opened and Leo Barany jumped out and frowned at Andrew. It could have been the sun in his eyes, but whatever the cause it wasn't much of a welcome. Andrew got out of his car and walked toward Leo.

"What can I do for you?" Barany asked angrily.

The Olds suddenly started to back up, and Leo had to jump out of the way. The woman was frantically turning the wheel, but not enough to avoid a sickening sideswipe of Andrew's Mercedes. This slowed her down some, but still in reverse careened out over the lawn. Barany ran after her and threw himself at the car. There was genuine terror on the woman's face now as she tried to steer the car and roll up the window at the same time. Barany clung to the car and got his upper body into the window.

Andrew stood frozen, watching the battered Olds go bouncing over the lawn toward the Wabash Road with the terrified woman at the wheel and Barany clinging to the car as if he meant to wrestle it to the ground. What the hell? Andrew began to run after the Olds himself.

The grille of the car lifted as it backed into the drainage ditch beside the road and came to a jolting stop when its rear end dug into the shoulder. Only Barany's legs hung out of the driver's window now. Andrew got to the car, grabbed the man's ankles and began to pull. Barany struggled to get a foot free and then began to kick out wildly. Andrew backed off.

Barany disappeared through the window, but the opposite door opened and the woman leapt out. She began to run up the road, blond hair bouncing, her arms and legs seeming to claw through the air. She hadn't gotten a good start before Barany was after her. Andrew, on the lawn, hesitated only a moment before going on the run to his car. He got the Mercedes started and made a big looping U-turn over the lawn, accelerated down the driveway, came spinning onto the Wabash Road, and took off after Barany.

It was the first chance he had to ask himself what was happening and he realized he had no answer. The woman was a waitress at the country club, he recognized her now, and there was no doubt that she was fleeing for her life.

She was running in a crazy zigzag way up the road, but moving at a good rate, her limbs under control now, arms tucked in. Nonetheless, Barany closed the distance between them easily, loping along without apparent effort. Andrew came along beside him, slowed the car to the bartender's speed, and began to ease him off the road.

Barany swung his clenched fist against the window of the Mercedes, his face grim with determination. He must be crazy. Did he think he could disable the car with his fist?

Andrew continued to pull to the left, forcing Barany to move with the car. He slowed and so did Andrew. He stopped dead and Andrew braked the Mercedes, which dipped its nose and stopped on a dime. Barany ducked out of sight, then rose suddenly, holding a boulder in both hands. Andrew accelerated but not fast enough. The boulder crashed against the back window and there was the sound of shattering glass.

Gunning the car, Andrew took off after the girl, who was fifty yards up the road and running faster than before, but as he neared her, she left the road in the direction of the golf course. He hit the horn, but she gestured to him without turning around. She wanted him to follow.

He pulled over to the side of the road, but before he got out of the car, Barany bounded across the drainage ditch and took off after the running girl. Andrew had no choice. He took off after them.

I'm no athlete, I'm a golfer. The punchline of the joke rang in his ears as he jogged after the couple, puffing now, a stitch in his side. It struck him that it would have made more sense to go for help. The thought slowed him, but then he saw that Barany had caught up with the girl, taken her by the arm, and was moving her through the trees away from the golf course. Then they stopped and seemed to be waiting for him as Andrew approached in a walk.

"What in the hell is going on?"

Barany's expression was one of almost detached calm, contrasting with the wild expression on the woman's face.

She stood slightly ahead of Barany and he seemed to have her arm twisted behind her.

"Throw down the keys to your car."

The command was so unexpected, Andrew just stared at the bartender. Just as he was about to lie and say he had left them in the car, the girl cried out in pain and leaned forward. Barany had increased the pressure on her arm. Andrew took the keys from his pocket and threw them on the ground.

Barany moved forward, pushing the girl ahead of him, and with the side of his foot sent the keys spinning into the bush.

"Very well, Mr. Broom. Start walking that way." He dipped his head to the right, and Andrew noticed that there was a yard beyond the trees that constituted the border of Walnut Grove Golf Course. Another cry of pain from the woman convinced him. He began to walk among the shaded trees in the direction of the yard, where grass and a small storage shed seemed to bake in the sun. He might have been in pursuit of a lost ball. But he was heading out of bounds.

"Where are we going, Barany?"

"Shut up and walk."

"He'll kill us!" the woman cried, and then again gave out a yelp of pain.

Andrew turned to see Barany bringing the woman's arm up higher behind her back. Her face was twisted in pain.

"You sonofabitch!"

Andrew lunged at Barany, pulling the girl free, lifting one arm to catch the downward movement of Barany's joined hands.

"Run!" he told the girl.

Barany's knee lifted, but Andrew turned away and caught the force of the blow in his upper thigh. God, what pain. He was pushed backward then, and one leg crumpled beneath him, disabled by the charley horse Barany's knee had caused. He was falling, and even as he fell Barany loomed over him like the menacing force of death itself. Barany's shoe dug into his side and Andrew tried to roll away from the pain. He managed to get to his hands and knees, but once more Barany kicked him in the side.

He was blacking out from the pain. What was he doing here? In his head he heard the girl cry *He'll kill us,* and he hoped she got away. Before he lost consciousness he had the crazy notion that he heard Gerald's voice and Cleary's, and he went out thinking that all would be well.

THIRTY-SIX

ONE OF THE PHONE NUMBERS scribbled on Slattery's bulletin board turned out to be Leo Barany's, which is what had brought Gerald and the sheriff to the house on the Wabash Road. They had knocked and rung and gone around back, which is where they had met Noreen Jensen.

"It was an adolescent's dream," Gerald mused. "This disheveled blond emerging from the woods, flinging herself into my arms."

He sat in the "parlor" in Andrew's office, enjoying an afternoon drink with his uncle and Susannah. A week had passed since the capture of Leo Barany or, as Gerald preferred putting it, the rescue of Noreen Jensen and Andrew Broom. Silvia Wood was doing well after her ordeal in the sheet-metal shed.

"Noreen would have been next," Susannah said, and shuddered.

"Then Andrew."

"Put a little feeling into that thought or I will change my will."

"Too bad about the Mercedes."

"I'm glad something tugs at your heart."

"Beside the disheveled blond," Susannah said.

"She might be what you are looking for, Gerald. Definitely an improvement over Julie McGough."

"In what way an improvement?"

"She runs faster."

"Julie doesn't run at all."

"You've grasped my point."

Susannah looked with concern at Andrew. He did not like to admit how much the struggle with Barany had cost him. But Susannah was determined he should take it easy for a while. Travel brochures of the Greek Isles were scattered on the round table before them. Gerald rose.

"Will you be back in time to defend Leo Barany?" Gerald asked with a straight face.

"I'll be back before the trial, but I won't be defending him. In fact, I suggested your name to Teufel."

Gerald stared at his uncle. He had to be kidding. But he never knew with Uncle Andrew.

"I'll have to disqualify myself."

"On what grounds?"

"I've fallen in love with one of the accused's victims."

"Gerald, I didn't realize you cared."

Susannah laughed, but then she was an easy audience for Andrew. Gerald turned on his heel and went off to keep his date with Julie.

Available in February.

A DEB RALSTON MYSTERY

DEATH WARMED OVER
LEE MARTIN

**NEITHER RAIN, NOR SNOW,
NOR SLEET, NOR HAIL...**

A postman is murdered in his van. Nearby sits a charred 1957 Chevy.
The first cop on the scene, Fort Worth Detective Deb Ralston is also the
first to find the abandoned house and the grisly bodies of a man and a
young girl.

It appeared to be a kidnapping gone sour—with $250,000 in ransom
money missing. But why try to burn the car? What had the postman
seen?

The suicide of the girl's mother reopens the bitter wounds of a long-
forgotten murder and points an accusing finger to people Deb Ralston
has known all her life. Soon she's unraveling a twisted skein of love,
hate and revenge that leads back to a Sunday churchyard . . . when all
hell broke loose.

Martin's "spirited, oft-put-upon detective is a revelation in the genre."
—*Booklist*

Available next month...

Hardball

Barbara D'Amato

A Cat Marsala Mystery

First
Time in
Paperback

FOR A SOFT-SPOKEN GRANDMOTHERLY TYPE, LOUISE SUGARMAN
HAD A LOT OF ENEMIES...

As head of Common Sense, an organization to repeal Illinois's
drug laws, Louise had earned the wrath of the PTA, police and
church groups all over Chicago. Free-lance journalist
Catherine Marsala smelled a great interview.

It was a bomb.

A bomb that killed Louise and almost killed Cat...in a room
packed with Sugarman's bitter opposition, including
Catherine's Uncle Ben, head of PASA, Parents Against
Substance Abuse.

Now Cat is hungry for more than a story...she wants to nail a
killer. Of course, the whole thing could win a Pulitzer...if she
lives long enough to write it.

"Cat Marsala is one of the most appealing new sleuths to
come along in years."   —Nancy Pickard

Available in March . . .

JAMES YAFFE

MOM MEETS HER MAKER

I HAD THE PERFECT GIFT FOR MOM THIS YEAR . . . A
MURDER. Not only was Dave's mother a great cook, she had
an amazing knack—between the chopped liver and the
strudel—for solving his most difficult murder cases. Possibly
because no detail, no matter how trivial, ever escaped that
rattrap brain of hers.

When the body of Reverend Chuck Candy is found three days
before Christmas, it's more than ill-timed murder. It's a
complex case of religious fanaticism, illicit affairs and small-
town bigotry. Dave—an investigator for the public defender—
believes an innocent man is being framed. And he knows only
one person in Mesa Grande, Colorado, can untangle the web
of unlikely connections and sinister intentions: Mom.

"Neat and trim, with a twist."—*New York Daily News*